PETER AND PAUL

Whether in her serious literary novels, her children's books, or the lighter romances written under the pseudonym Susan Scarlett, Noel Streatfeild wrote about what she knew, and put to good use the experiences of her early home life and career. So from her vicarage upbringing we have *Parson's Nine*, *Under the Rainbow*, *Peter and Paul* and *The Bell Family*. From her work in munitions at the Woolwich Arsenal in World War I we gain *Murder While You Work*. From her social work in Deptford came *Tops and Bottoms,* and her extensive war work in Civil Defence and the WVS went into *I Ordered a Table for Six, Saplings* and *When the Siren Wailed.* There was even a short spell of modelling which she used in *Clothes-Pegs* and *Peter and Paul.* And then there was the theatre, where her ten year acting career embraced many branches of the profession. Chorus girls and concert parties (*It Pays to be Good, Poppies for England*), pantomime, with its troupe of children, (*Wintle's Wonders*), ballet training (*Ballet Shoes, Pirouette*), a touring Shakespeare company and her eventual disillusionment with the profession (*The Whicharts*) - all of these found their way into her books. She had a long and distinguished literary career with 90 books, the Carnegie Medal and an O.B.E. to her credit.

PETER AND PAUL

SUSAN SCARLETT

Greyladies

Published by
Greyladies
an imprint of The Old Children's Bookshelf
175 Canongate, Edinburgh EH8 8BN

© Noel Streatfeild 1940
This edition first published 2010
Design and layout © Shirley Neilson 2010

ISBN   978-1-907503-05-4

Set in Sylfaen / Perpetua

Printed in Great Britain by the
MPG Books Group, Bodmin and King's Lynn

PETER AND PAUL

CHAPTER 1

PAULINE AND PETRONELLA sat side by side. They were in church. They looked up at their father who was preaching. They both had absorbed expressions. Pauline because she was listening to the sermon. Petronella because she had been brought up in a vicarage, and since the age of six had learnt the knack of wearing the look parishioners expect parson's daughters to have in church. The expression on Petronella's face had nothing to do with what was in her mind. At the moment she was thinking of clothes. She had on a green artificial silk frock. Petronella's was a soul which without training abhorred artificial silks. "Oh, goodness," she thought, "if only I could have a real heavy *crêpe de Chine.*"

Pauline, totally unconscious that her blue frock was not only artificial silk, but faded a little as well, was following every word of her father's sermon. It was the sort of sermon she liked best. He was preaching on the parable of the grain of mustard seed. "The kingdom of heaven is like to a grain of mustard seed, which a man took and sowed in a field; which indeed is the least of all seeds; but when it is grown, it is the greatest among herbs . . ."

It is not fun being the plain one of the family. But being the plain one of twins is a wretched position. That's why parables about grains of mustard seed, which grew up and startled everybody by their magnificence, did Pauline good.

On the outside of the pew sat Catherine Lane, the twins' mother. Catherine had been born a Marchant. The

1

Marchants were not millionaires, but they were that kind of rich which made it unnecessary to think much about what was being spent. Catherine knew just what she was doing when she married Mark Lane. She was so in love that she could not have helped marrying him even if he had less than he had; though that was practically impossible. Though her husband would always come first in her life, she had been terribly pleased to have twins. She had thought it would be amusing having two little girls exactly alike to dress alike. But that's where she was entirely wrong. Almost from the day they were born the difference had been apparent. Pauline had been a perfect baby. She lay for hours sleeping and cooing in her cot. Petronella had been a terror. She had screamed at the slightest discomfort or inconvenience, and bellowed when bored. Then as they grew fatter and rounder there were other differences. Pauline was an enchanting baby. Just a nice, normal baby, such as any home expected and adored. But Petronella was like something out of a fairy-story. Pauline had straight, fair hair. Petronella had hair the colour of a pale primrose, and it curled like the tendrils on a sweet-pea. Both twins had blue eyes. But Pauline's were just blue. Petronella's were like lapis lazuli. Often when there had been visitors or relations in the house Catherine would hurry off to the village shop and come running back with a rattle or other little toy for Pauline. Even a baby, she thought, must notice it when she got just affectionate pats and her sister was surrounded by a worshipping crowd.

As they grew older the differences between the sisters grew more marked. Petronella was slim, with a figure which at all ages was perfect. Pauline had her awkward periods. Petronella had enough charm to sink a battleship. It did not seem to matter what she left undone, there was always someone to do things for her. Pauline had a quiet depth of character, based on lovely qualities of which Petronella had never heard. But owing to some injustice in human make-up, people took advantage of Pauline's niceness and made her do dull, uninteresting jobs for them. It was the custom all over the parish to hand Petronella slices of cake or plates of strawberries to amuse her, while Pauline bandaged cuts, looked through the accounts, or delivered magazines.

Now they were seventeen. Catherine shifted her position slightly in her pew. She tried to focus on what Mark was saying, but it was impossible. How can you focus on hyperthetical grains of mustard seed, when this very day you are trying to plant your own two seeds out in the world?

It had taken Catherine weeks to get to the point of asking Lady Bliss a favour. But really when you have two daughters in a small village somebody has got to do something. Mark was so tiresome. Angelic though Catherine thought him, she did wish sometimes that he was a shade more worldly. It seemed incredible in the twentieth century that there could be a man who thought futures for daughters would just work out in the natural scheme of things. He must see as he ground his way round his parish in their deplorable old Morris, that there was not a marriageable man within miles. He read the papers, and so must have grasped that the extraordinary way in which he had insisted on the girls being brought up was not the way in which to fit them for careers. They had none of those school certificates or head mistresses' reports which opened office doors and made business houses consider engagements. That was why she had dared to go to Lady Bliss. Lady Bliss had valuable connections. It was one of the connections, a nephew, that she had sent for this afternoon. "David," she said, "has a dressmaking business. Rotten work for a man. But he makes a lot of money. He shall take the girls." Catherine could not imagine why the unfortunate David should take two totally untrained girls, but if Lady Bliss said he would then it was almost certain he would. She was not the kind of woman to whom anybody said "No." Catherine heaved a sigh of relief. How lucky Lady Bliss was fond of Mark. Not that there could be anybody who was not fond of Mark. All the same it was lucky Lady Bliss was, for the girls must get away. They must meet people. Catherine clasped her hands. "And, oh, please, heaven, let them meet men as fine as their father."

Lady Bliss sat with her eyes shut. As a rule she slept during the sermon and called it meditating. To-day she was really meditating. She was thinking of David Bliss. David was her eldest brother-in-law's boy, and the eldest brother-in-law had been killed in the war. That had made David a special care with all the family. She had done more than just care. The death of her husband and David's mother marrying again had almost coincided. What more natural that a rich, desperately unhappy widow, should make a second home for a small nephew, who was in a mood bordering on frenzy because of jealousy of a stepfather? Perhaps it had been the stepfather coming into his life at just that moment had made David turn contrary. He had brains and money. He was sent to Winchester and Oxford, where he did brilliantly and started coaching for the diplomatic. Then without warning to anybody he threw it all up and said he was off to Paris to study dress-designing. Everybody blamed him except Lady Bliss. She was sorry, but she was not alienating an adored nephew by saying so. She grasped that perhaps at a highly strained moment an over-pompous stepfather had said, "We all expect splendid things of you, my boy." To which David had retorted, "Do you! Then I'm damned if you'll get them."

It was nice she had the excuse of the twins to get him down to-day. With the enormously successful "Reboux" to run he was hard to get hold of. Of course, now that that quite immoral, but highly efficient creature, Moira Renton, was managing for him he was a bit more free. But then he was so keen on games. What with his polo and golf, and cricket tours there was not much time for him to come and call on an old aunt. Nor would he be pleased when she told him what she wanted. No smart dressmaker with a complete staff wants twins from a country vicarage foisted on him. But he would give in. She would insist. That enchanting creature, Catherine, was looking quite drawn. No wonder. It must be a terrible strain trying to make two ends meet. Then the girls were a worry. That lovely little creature, Petronella, demanding money the whole time to go to the cinema and other nonsense. Wretched occupations for the child, but really you could not blame her. Except for an occasional very dull garden party or tennis-party there were no amusements in Farlynge, and even at those entertainments no men anywhere near the girls' ages. It was easier, of course, with Pauline. She was nearly as great a dear as her mother and that was saying a lot.

Pauline would find things to do on an uninhabited rock. But she should not be put to it. As nice a girl as that should have chances to meet men. It would be a tragedy if someone with such wells of happiness to give, missed the man she was meant to love.

Lady Bliss heard a rustle behind her. She pulled herself together, prepared to stand up for the Blessing, but it was a false alarm. Mark was just describing the first leaves on the mustard plant. There was still some way to go. She settled back again. She wondered if she dared tackle David on the subject of Moira Renton.

Moira Renton was one of those women whom everybody of her world had known since she was born. Her birth had made front-page news in the evening papers. Her christening a month later in one of the most exclusive fonts was on the news reels. Neither her father nor mother, Lord and Lady Belton, ever wanted Moira to be news, but she just was. Through her babyhood she was photographed in her perambulator in the park. As soon as she could toddle every paper had enormous photos of the Honourable Moira Belton as a bridesmaid. Throughout her childhood she was so often a bridesmaid that when at eighteen she was presented her face was familiar to everyone who looks at picture papers. It was like the presentation of a close friend. All this press did not matter as long as Moira was a child. Whatever her nurses, governesses, and school mistresses might think of her there was always the hope she might improve in time. In any case her worst qualities were hidden behind nursery and schoolroom walls. But out in the great world it was different. She had scarcely made her curtsy, and her maid packed away her feathers and train before gossip began to circulate. "Now there is gossip and gossip," as Lady Belton said gloomily to her husband, " but the sort dear Moira is attracting is, to say the least of it, unfortunate."

The trying part, as nobody knew better than the Beltons, was that Moira was not wholly to blame. As a race they were fined down by inter-breeding. They were brilliant, brittle and effete. Without excitement of some sort, Moira was a dead thing. With excitement she flamed as though a match had been thrown among wood shavings. At the age of twenty-three there was probably no means to stimulate excitement with which Moira had not experimented. The life she led cost an appalling amount of money. The Beltons were not rich, as their world counted money, they were poor. Time and again something was sold to keep Moira out of the bankruptcy courts. But at twenty-three there was nothing left that could raise money in a hurry. Moira had no wish to go bankrupt, she said, "It made shops so tiresome about bills afterwards." She looked round for some sort of life-belt. Her eye lighted on Tommy Renton.

Tommy Renton was the nice, good-looking son of a chain of stores. He was the sort of person who makes the world say that England would not stand where it does, if it were not for the great middle classes. He was extraordinarily nice and extraordinarily rich. Moira had fascinated him from a distance for some time. When she came nearer he could not believe his luck. He, simple Tommy Renton, to marry this dream of loveliness.

For quite a while Tommy believed he had found happiness. Believed it in spite of everything. Then one day something came under his nose which even his blind love could not fail to notice. He took a train to Eastbourne. He fell over Beachy Head. The Coroner brought in that the death took place while he was temporarily insane. This was probably true. England hissed with whispers. Moira found herself up against it. Tommy had been too nice, and what Tommy had discovered, too unpleasant. Moira's maid packed hurriedly, and Moira went to America.

It was while Moira was in America that David Bliss's dress shop, "Reboux", became really famous. So famous that women in New York going to and fro to Europe said, "Oh, and my dear, I got three or four things from "Reboux" that are "just darling." Moira listened to all this and saw the clothes were " just darling ", though that was not the way she would have put it herself. She had her big idea. She knew David, they belonged to the same world. She had been very attracted by him, and he by her. In fact, looking over the past she wondered why the attraction had not been allowed to run its course — or had it? It was so difficult after a year or two to remember what you had done, with whom, and when. Anyway in David, or rather in "Reboux", she saw her way back to London. From passing friends she learnt that he had no manageress. From her knowledge of him she knew this must be rectified in time. A man like David who could not be happy unless he was hitting some sort of ball about, must want someone smart and competent he could leave the business to, off and on.

David was a good business man. Moira's letter coincided with a restive moment when he was feeling too tied down. He sent her a cable.

The return of Moira to England and her appearance at

"Reboux" was news. "Reboux" was crowded. Everybody decided it was just the moment to order something new, and they all came, and whispered over cocktails how Moira looked. "Not a bit changed, my dear. She must be hard as granite. Anyone with any heart would never look people in the face again." And some said, "Lucky for Moira she's hit on that job. She'll need it." For Tommy, before he went over Beachy Head, had not been too insane to see his lawyers. He had not left Moira his fortune. He left her what to most people would have been a decent income, to her it was pin money, and pin money which she resented. "Anybody who wasn't a cad would have left me the lot," she told her maid bitterly. Her maid, who had liked Tommy, said nothing.

Moira enjoyed being at "Reboux". It is always fun to find you have a gift. Moira found she had one for selling clothes. She picked up, more or less, with her old world. She had lovely clothes ("Reboux" dressed her, it was part of the contract). She had a very good commission on all the stock. And since no money (however much) was really enough to keep her, she, as well, slightly falsified the books, which she kept. The prices she entered at which the clothes were sold were several pounds out from the price she really got for them. The difference went into Moira's bank

One thing Moira found wrong with her world. Even after four years of working for David she was not really rehabilitated with the people who mattered. Not the rich, raffish crowd—they were easy—but the die-hard aristocracy to which she really belonged. As she grew older this riled her more and more. To herself she said, "What the hell do they matter, anyway! Lot of dreary old frumps."

But she did mind. And she decided to put things straight. She would marry David.

It was this idea of marriage that made Lady Bliss, who was no fool, put the rest of the time Mark preached to David's future. As a show-woman, saleswoman and manageress at "Reboux", yes. An admirable arrangement. The creature had poise, beauty, and somewhere breeding. She supposed that since fate took her and David about together a good deal she was other things to him as well. In this she was wrong. But she was not wrong in what her shrewd old eyes had seen—a certain bitterness when invitations were issued to parties at which the names of those invited had to be submitted to very important people indeed. Moira would laugh and say lightly that those sort of parties were deadly anyway. But Lady Bliss was not deceived. As you got older the wish to be established appealed more. Moira must be twenty-seven or twenty-eight. She wanted to settle down. Not really settle, of course—at seventy Moira would not do that. But, at least, have the outward semblance of a background. And what could be better for her purpose than David. David who was so used to her he might not think marriage a bad idea.

Mark turned his back to the congregation, which rose hurriedly and clatteringly to its feet. He gave the Gloria.

"I shall sound David," said Lady Bliss to herself. "He has no father. I can't have him falling into the hands of that harpy."

No one, thought Petronella, knew how awful it was for a girl not to have enough hats. Hats were really more important than anything else. That is, if you had nice legs, which she had. Of course, it was awful having to wear artificial silk. If ever a girl was born to wear the best of everything, she was. Still, even artificial silk does not look bad if your legs are good. But hats! The sort of hats she and Pauline had to wear simply smelt of vicarages. They weren't a bit the sort of hats people like Greta Garbo wore. It didn't matter so much to Pauline, because she never could look like a film star anyway. But she did look like one. She'd put photographs of people like Claudette Colbert and Deanna Durbin up against hers in front of the looking-glass, and so she knew. In lots of ways she thought hers was a better face. Only, of course, it looked wrong in the wrong hats.

It was these thoughts which kept Petronella, walking down the lane after Sunday lunch. She had to think hard how badly treated she was about hats or she would have felt like a criminal. Because in her hand was a parcel. The goods in the parcel were to be exchanged with Miss Rosalie. Miss Rosalie made hats all the week for a firm in Brighton. Anybody, thought Petronella, who made hats in Brighton must know all there was to know about hats. Even the thought of a new hat could not entirely cheer her up. She was, she was sure, committing an unusually un-pleasant sin. Surely no vicar's daughter had ever before traded a new hat for six hymn-books. Not *Ancient and Modern*, for those would be missed, but six of the *Church Hymnals*, which were not used now and lived in the attic. Miss Rosalie liked the *Church Hymnals* best. She said that at "her little mission" they went with more of a swing. Petronella had never seen Miss Rosalie's Sunday Evening Mission, with Miss Rosalie at the piano leading the singing in her shrill, sing-song voice, but she was thankful *Church Hymnals* would do.

At the end of the lane, where she should climb a style to get to Miss Rosalie's little house, she stopped. She took a piece of mirror out of her pocket. She stared at her face. Then she looked at her parcel. Then she climbed the style.

"It shall have a veil," she promised herself, and then added devoutly, "I'm sure I shall feel a much better church woman in a veil."

On the lawn at the Vicarage, Catherine stretched herself out flat in a deck-chair. Pauline lay on a rug beside her.

"One of the things I am most thankful for," said Catherine, "is that your father never wanted me to teach in Sunday-school. Everybody has bits of time they cherish. I cherish Sunday afternoons."

Pauline rolled over on to her tummy and considered the point.

"I like all time. I don't believe one bit's nicer than another."

"That, my child," Catherine retorted severely, "is because you are blessed with a nice disposition like your father's. I remember I once said to him, 'What time of day do you like best?' And he said, 'The mornings. A new day of service before me'." She looked affectionately at her pinks flowering round her rose-beds. "I can't think why it is parsons can get away with saying things which would make anyone else sound like the most awful prig."

Pauline stretched out her hand and collected a mass of dark red petals which had fallen off a rose.

"It's because they mean it, I think." She listened. "Bother, there's the telephone!" She got up.

Catherine looked at her.

"Now look, darling, unless it's a death, don't let anyone see Daddy to-day. You know how tired he is on Sundays. But if it's Mrs. Caldicott to say I can have a box of nemesias, say we'll come over for them at once. She is so fond of promising the same plants to more than one person. It may be unchristian, but if anyone is going to have those nemesias it's me."

Pauline was only gone a few minutes. She came flying back across the lawn. She knelt down by Catherine's chair.

"Darling, what have you been up to?"

In a flash Catherine knew the call must have been from Lady Bliss.

"Nothing, why?"

Pauline grinned at her affectionately.

"Come out with it. Lady Bliss says to tell you she thinks it's all right. And will you please bring both of us to tea this afternoon to see David."

Catherine sighed. The moment for explaining her schemes was obviously on her.

"Well, he's got a dressmaking business. I want him to give you two some work."

Pauline stared at her mother.

"Why! I'm happy here. And I'm awfully useful. Look at all the things I run for Daddy."

"Far too many." Catherine patted the hand that Pauline in her anxiety had laid on her knee. "The world is full of spinsters who have become extra curates to some parson. I don't intend you to be one of them."

"But why dressmaking?"

13

Catherine's eyes twinkled

"Your father didn't approve of higher, or even lower education for you girls. I've taught you to read and write, and to talk French. And your father has taught you Greek and Latin. You're dreadfully ignorant. The most inefficient office in the world wouldn't look at either of you."

"We learnt history and arithmetic and things from Mr. Smith."

Catherine smiled reminiscently at the picture of Mr. Smith, the village schoolmaster. He had arrived on his bicycle every day after school hours, dusty and tired, his trousers rather ridiculously held in with bicycle clips.

"You know you never learnt anything from him. You always put him under a tree in the summer, and by the fire in the winter, and gave him enormous teas."

"Well, I think he was hungry, poor little man." Pauline's face clouded at the memory. "Nobody could be so mean as to want a man who was hungry to teach them geography. And Petronella wouldn't have learnt anyway. She always said she wouldn't learn after tea."

"Or before tea. Or any other time." Catherine sat up. "By the way, where is Petronella?"

Pauline picked up the rose petals again. She squeezed them till they smelt.

"Is it a bought tell?"

A "bought tell" was a hang-over from the twins' childhood. If a grown-up asked for information and said they bought it, then whatever crime they heard of they could not punish for it. It was "bought" and therefore paid for.

Catherine nodded.

"All right."

"Well, she's gone to Miss Rosalie. She's going to have a hat in exchange for six of those old hymnbooks in the attic."

"Really!" Catherine looked shocked. "As if your father wouldn't gladly have given Miss Rosalie a dozen of those hymn-books for her funny little mission. Petronella must take that hat straight back."

Pauline held up a reminding finger.

"It was a bought tell. Besides I've only guessed. I saw Petronella pack the books and go out and I knew Miss Rosalie wanted them."

"Well, if you knew she wanted them why didn't you give them to her for nothing?"

"Petronella wanted a hat. She's very pretty. She needs hats and things."

A slightly worried frown flicked across Catherine's face.

"Is there anything you wouldn't do for Petronella?"

Pauline stared at the garden. At the round beds of roses surrounded by pinks. At the herbaceous border. At the old weather-mellowed walls of the Vicarage with the fuchsia standing in the corner.

"No, I don't think so."

"Neither do I," said Catherine, "but I wish it wasn't true."

"It is a pity," said Catherine, as she and Pauline walked up the drive to the Manor House, "that your father had to preach at Foxborough this afternoon, otherwise we could have had the car and have fetched Petronella. I do hope David will engage both of you only seeing one of you."

"He knows what we look like. At least he ought to. He saw us every Sunday for holiday after holiday."

15

"The last time he saw you two you were eight." Catherine paused to admire an azalea. "I wish your father was rich and I could have a gardener with nothing to do but grow orange, sticky azaleas."

"Heavenly! What a pity it's me he's got to see and not Petronella. Why didn't you tell us you had fearful schemes of selling us to a dressmaking shop, then Petronella would have stayed in."

They turned the corner. The Manor House lay in front of them in its almost un-altered sixteenth-century grace. Catherine did not answer until she had taken a long look at it. Beauty, she said, was more of a pick-me-up than any tonic.

"I suppose," she explained at last, "I hadn't thought of his wanting to see you. After all, neither of you can sew much, so I thought you were better sold off as pigs in pokes, as it were. It's so lucky Lady Bliss is fond enough of your father to want to help."

Pauline looked up at her mother. A quick feeling of love shot over her. It was so sharp it almost hurt. Was there another woman in the world as much loved as Catherine who did not know it?

Lady Bliss was in her drawing-room. An extraordinarily Edwardian affair of occasional tables, signed photographs in massive silver frames of the royal family, large rose-bowls tumbling with gardener-selected roses, really good family portraits cheek by jowl with quite shocking ones, and cabinets of good, or near good, glass and china, and a mantelpiece surrounded by some very delicate silhouettes. She kissed Catherine on both cheeks.

"How are you, my dear? Where's Petronella? Well, I dare

say it doesn't matter. I've told David she's grown into a beauty. He says if it's true she can model clothes. No, dear, you wouldn't know what that was, bless you. You never wore a frock in your life that was worth modelling. Pauline, my dear, David's down by the river, I think. Go and find him and bring him back to tea. Whatever you do don't tell him you can't sew. Now, Catherine, come straight out to the rose garden and tell me why my roses get black spot and yours don't."

David was not fishing. His aunt never allowed anything to be killed on her property on Sundays. But that did not prevent anyone who was fond of fishing lying on his face and looking at the trout where they lay under the bank

David never had thought of his appearance. He knew he was fair and thin, and six foot two, and that was about all. He did not know that he had grey-blue eyes which could change with amazing rapidity from crinkled amusement to absorbed interest, and just once in a while to tenderness. He had never thought of his hands so he did not know that every inch of his creative ability showed in his over-long, sensitive, brown fingers. He never thought of figures so his (with its apparent laziness which turned to agility and grace when there was anything to be done) never crossed his mind. He never thought of lines except on a woman, and so it never struck him that his lack of hips and incredible length of leg had made more women than Moira hint, "It wouldn't be at all a bad idea."

Pauline found him stretched out full length. He might not have noticed her when she was eight, but she had seen him almost every holiday while he was at Winchester. Right up to the moment when he had rebelled at too much

17

of his aunt and church and had wanted to go on cricket tours and play in golf matches and do anything, in fact, except spend his Sundays sitting in Farlynge Church, and escorting his aunt round the Manor gardens afterwards. Not that he was not devoted to his aunt. He was. Only there comes a time when a man must come and go at his own pleasure. He came and went a lot at that, but Pauline had never happened to see him.

Pauline looked at him now in pained surprise.

"That suit's much too good to lie about in," she said. "It's nearly always damp by the river and I expect you'll get green marks."

He sat up.

"The nice twin?"

Pauline found a dry tree-trunk and sat down beside him.

"Petronella's as nice as me. She's the pretty one."

David felt an odd stirring of tenderness in his heart. He looked at Pauline's charming little face. At the tip-tilted nose. The generous mouth. The level eyes that could not lie to a person. This was not the lovely twin, of course. His aunt was no fool. When she said lovely, she meant it. He had been furious at having what he described as "two prunes and prisms from a vicarage" foisted on him. Now, looking at Pauline, he wondered if there might not be points in the arrangement.

"I expect you're hating us," said Pauline sympathetically. "It must be awful to have twins handed you suddenly. I hope we'll make clothes nicely. We've only made them for heathen before. You know, working parties for foreign missions. But I expect we'll learn."

"Not on my clothes, you won't."

18

Pauline looked relieved.

"Oh, that's good. I don't want to be a dressmaker really. It was Mother's idea. She was afraid of me being a sort of extra curate. Spinsters are sometimes."

"There are other jobs besides making clothes. You might sell them."

"Might I!" Pauline considered the idea. "I shouldn't think I'd be very good at it. You see, we've never had any clothes so I don't know much about them. Do you remember those awful little green coats we used to wear in church?"

David smoked happily.

"No, I remember dresses all puckered in front."

"Smocked," said Pauline. "A man who designs dresses ought to know that."

David went on as if she had not spoken.

"You had big hats, and on one of you, the fairest curls I've ever seen stuck out from underneath."

"Petronella," Pauline sighed resignedly. "It's a pity to be the plain one of twins. All my life things like Petronella's curls are what people remember."

David gave her a quick look.

"Nobody could call you plain."

"Oh, yes, they could." Pauline got up and smoothed her frock. "It's tea-time. If you've a twin like Petronella, that's what they call you all the time."

He got up and stood beside her.

"I'm glad you're coming to work for me."

"Are you? " Pauline looked at him surprised. "I shan't be much use."

David looked over her head. The beech trees were that piercing green of early June. The bracken had hardly

19

uncurled. Everything looked very young and fresh. So young and fresh that thoughts of Moira and marriage which had lately been buzzing in his head seemed sordid. Yesterday, even to-day, the thought of marrying her had been in his mind. He did not love her, who could who knew her, but she was an amusing companion, and as far as business was concerned they were tied anyway. But now, with all this freshness, and that something in Pauline which made you feel you were out in the early morning, while the dew was still on the grass, his vision changed. He straightened his back and smiled at her.

"I dare say you'll be a wonder at sewing on buttons when put to it. But there are more uses for a twin than are dreamed of in your philosophy, my child. Come on. Let's ruin our figures on scones and honey."

Being in love has nothing to do with age. It can catch you without a morsel of warning at seventeen, twenty-seven, thirty-seven, forty-seven. Always, in fact, while you've pulses to beat. But at seventeen it arrives as a stranger. The signs are new. The fact that suddenly the whole world has changed its shape is inexplicable. It takes experience and suffering to say, "Oh, heavens, I'm in love."

Pauline, walking up through the wood beside David, was amazed. Had the sky turned bluer? Had the birds always sung so loudly? Did bracken always smell so lovely? Crossing the lawn she gasped at the scent of the roses. She was so surprised by the radiance of the world that she looked quite dazed as she followed David in through the french windows.

Catherine loved both her daughters, but in her

innermost heart she loved Pauline best. She did not, of course, actually admit it ever, but it was one of those things she knew she would find if ever she had to turn out her heart and lay its secrets on a metaphorical table. It was, therefore, discouraging how often Pauline let her down. Petronella had the looks, there was no getting away from that, but Pauline could try harder. She need not as now (practically the only time when she was with a nice-looking man) appear suddenly half-witted. There was really a gorgeous tea. Why must Pauline, who usually liked nice things to eat, look at the food handed to her as if it was not there?

"Has David told you," Lady Bliss said to Pauline, "that he's making places at 'Reboux' for both you and Petronella? Nothing big to start with, of course, but you never know. Do you, David? They might turn out to be marvellous, mightn't they?" David grunted in agreement so his aunt rattled on. "And I've just been telling your mother I know of a perfectly charming place where you can stay, except at the week-ends, of course, when you'll come home. I'm sure your dear father wouldn't dream of allowing you to be away on Sundays, and quite right too. Why, I had a niece who was away every Sunday and that was why, I am sure, things turned out as they did. Sundays can be so dull, especially in the winter, and you must do something. Anyway, it was a very nice baby and they're married now."

David looked at Catherine.

"The sort of terrifying experiences my aunt suggests never occur at my shop." He helped himself to another scone. "Where are you putting the twins, aunt?"

"Oh, my dear," Lady Bliss settled comfortably in her

chair. "Do you remember that nice creature, Miss Williams, I had to look after you when you were a little boy? Well, she's running a club for girls now. Very nice, and so well organized."

David made a face.

"What! That creature with the teeth that stuck out." He turned to Pauline. "I should refuse. She was a repulsive hag."

Pauline smiled. She did not care what David said as long as he spoke.

"Perhaps she's nicer now."

David shook his head.

"Once a hag, always a hag, that's my motto. But you can start there. One of the other girls, or Mrs. Renton, my manageress, may know of something better for later on."

At the words "Mrs. Renton", Lady Bliss's face set in lines of disapproval. It was an expression David had known since he was a little boy. When his aunt got that look any hope of wheedling was over, and punishment might be imminent. Catherine knew the look. It was the sort Lady Bliss wore when she thought Mark was getting "Popish". It meant that whatever innovation Mark wanted would be won over Lady Bliss's dead body. "It was no good, darling," Mark would say to Catherine, "she had on her 'Scarlet Woman' face." Pauline had not seen the look before, but she felt it was directed at David. Nobody ought to look at David like that.

"I'm sure that will be awfully nice," she broke in quickly. "It will be very kind of Mrs. Renton."

All through lunch, and all the afternoon, Lady Bliss had skirted the subject of Moira, only to be checkmated by

David. Now she could hold herself in no longer.

"Mrs. Renton is a person," she said icily, "who is admirable in her sphere of managing a business for David, but is not one with whom one would wish to discuss one's domestic arrangements, or in any way meet socially."

Catherine blinked. In her innocence, locked since her eighteenth birthday in a world bounded by vicarage walls, she had never heard of Moira or her kind. And if she had, would probably have said, "I don't expect half of it's true. People have such unkind tongues." But in any case, whatever Mrs. Renton might or might not be, Miss Williams was obviously the person she needed just now. It was going to be hard enough making Mark allow the girls to go to London at all. That they were to stay with someone who had once been a nursery governess at the Manor would at least help. She smiled at Lady Bliss and asked for the address.

Lady Bliss and Catherine walked to the gates together. Lady Bliss wanted to show Catherine how well her rhododendrons were doing. Catherine wanted to glean courage for her coming talk with Mark. When she had asked for help about the girls she had never thought of it all happening in such a hurry. Never in her wildest dreams had she pictured them working and settled in London in a fortnight, but that was what had happened. Monday week, David had said. At the thought of what Mark would say about Monday week, or Monday year if it came to that, her courage ran out of her toes.

Lady Bliss stopped beside a rhododendron which was as pink as a sunset.

"Thank goodness this 'Pink Pearl' has pulled itself

together. It looked terrible in the spring. I thought it was done for." She laid a hand on Catherine's arm. "All women, my dear, have to take sides now and again between their children and their husband. Mark's a great dear and a saint. In fact, so much of a saint that if he wasn't a great dear he'd be a prig. But even saints want keeping in their places now and then. Those children of yours have not had the upbringing they might have had because Mark thinks a woman's place is in the home. You who mix admirable common sense with your godliness have a duty to do."

Catherine looked depressed.

"If you only knew how difficult Mark is to persuade into doing things he's not sure are right. Besides, he's never grasped that the girls are growing up."

"No man ever thinks his daughters are grown up, and no woman that her sons are. But thinking never altered things."

"You're quite right." Catherine straightened her shoulders. "I'm a miserable, cowardly creature. But the children shall be at 'Reboux' on Monday week, and bless you for giving them the chance."

Lady Bliss moved on.

"If there's any blessing to be done it's by me, my dear. I'm fond of you, Catherine."

Catherine flushed.

"That's because I'm Mark's wife. People get quite to like me because I belong to him."

David and Pauline walked to the gates together.

"Was it fun," asked Pauline, "when you stayed here when you were little?"

David looked back over the years.

"At first it was, when I was quite small. My father used to come, too. He taught me to ride."

"He was killed in the war, wasn't he? It's to him Lady Bliss put up the window in the church. Were you miserable after that?"

"Not because of my father. I was too small to realize really. But afterwards" — his voice grew bitter — "when my mother married again. I hated my stepfather."

"Was he awful?"

He laughed.

"Not really, I suppose. Just a man like the rest of us. But he took my mother away from me. I couldn't understand, and I loathed him for it."

"Poor little boy," said Pauline indignantly. "What a shame! I think if people marry twice they ought always to think of their children first, don't you?"

His eyes twinkled

"I suspect, Twin, you are not speaking from great depths of experience. It mightn't be as easy as all that."

She looked at him puzzled.

"You mean loving a person very much makes you only think about them."

He nodded.

"I've never been in love. At least, not quite like that. But I suspect that's the answer."

They walked a little way in silence. Then Pauline asked:

"After a bit, when you'd got used to the stepfather, were you happier here?"

"Oh, yes, it became home. I had my dogs, and two ferrets, and my guns and fishing things, and I played for the village at cricket in the summer holidays. There isn't an inch of the place I don't know."

"And all the time I was little," said Pauline regretfully; "— only eight when you went away."

He stopped and held her elbow.

"Funny Twin. You sound quite sad about it."

"I am." Pauline looked up at him. "I'd like to have known you when you were little."

He went on standing and holding her elbow. There was something very warming about Pauline. She had about her a quality which made you think of eggs waiting by a hot fire after a long day's hunting. Of simple jokes shared. Of unfailing wisdom, so that no matter what mess you got into she would always make it seem less terrible than it was and find the way out.

There were footsteps down the path. Catherine and Lady Bliss came towards them. David dropped Pauline's arm and wondered why he had been holding it.

"Sorry," he said. "Don't know why I was boring you with stories of me as a kid."

Pauline's voice rang with truth.

"But I loved it."

He moved on.

"Well, now, you shall see me as a full-grown business man. Monday week."

"Monday week," Pauline agreed.

CHAPTER 2

"WHY," ASKED CATHERINE, as she and Pauline walked home, "are you holding your elbow? Have you knocked it?"

Pauline let go of her elbow as if it had stung her.

"No—I mean I didn't know I was—I mean—"

"Of course," Catherine went on, not noticing Pauline's prevarications, "you mustn't say a word to your father about this. I'll tell him after supper. You can tell Petronella. But don't say a word until she promises to keep it to herself."

Pauline moved to the bank and picked a handful of buttercups and cow parsley.

"All right, I promise." Then she looked at her mother. "Sooner you than me to tell Daddy. I bet he won't like it."

"So do I," Catherine agreed. Then she added with dignity, "But it's my duty."

Pauline giggled.

"I bet Lady Bliss said that. It doesn't sound a bit like you."

Petronella was sitting on a deck-chair on the lawn. She looked self-conscious.

"Well, where is it?" said Catherine.

Petronella opened what were meant to be surprised eyes. It never mattered much what Petronella meant her eyes to express, for whoever looked into them was lost in their blueness, and positively tangled in the length of her eye-lashes.

"Where's what?"

"The hat."

Petronella looked reproachfully at Pauline.

"Did you guess? You needn't have told anyway."

"She asked me where you were," Pauline explained. "Anyhow, it's a 'bought'."

"Oh"—Petronella got up—"in that case, I'll show you the hat. I look like Marlene Dietrich in it."

The hat in which Petronella reappeared was large and black. It was tied under her chin with black velvet ribbons. Over it was hung a large veil.

"Goodness," said Pauline. "You look like Mrs. Forbes when she was at her husband's funeral."

Catherine examined the creation critically.

"You do look like Marlene Dietrich. But then she doesn't live in a country vicarage. If you must copy film stars, couldn't you choose a less dashing one?"

Petronella sighed at the stupidity of parents.

"One must dress to type."

"Well, I do hope, darling, you won't wear it outside the garden. That time you changed your hair and wouldn't wear a hat, practically everybody in the parish came and asked if you were ill."

"People are very ignorant," said Petronella. "Just because I look like Jean Arthur I needn't be ill."

"We're lucky," Pauline pointed out to Catherine, "that she doesn't think she looks like Shirley Temple. It really would upset the parish if she wore skirts up to her middle, and socks."

Catherine turned towards the house.

"It's church time. I do hope they sing 'Fight the Good Fight' or something bracing. I'm naturally born to think rocks of ages were cleft for me, so that sort of hymn weakens my resistance."

"What does Mum want to resist about?" asked Petronella.

Pauline sat down on the lawn.

"I'm only to tell you if you promise not to say anything about it until Mum's told Daddy."

"All right."

"No," Pauline shook her head. "It's important. You'd better swear."

Petronella got unwillingly out of her chair. She took off the precious hat. She touched her forehead.

"I-swear-by-us-being-twins-never-to-say-what-I-shall-now-hear-so-help-me-God." She put her hat on again and sat down. "Now what is it?"

"Well," said Pauline, "you better hold on to something, because you're going to be awfully surprised. We're going to live in London and work in a dress-shop."

Petronella had spent a mass of time inventing futures for herself. She had mentally been almost everything from Queen of England, to a nurse dying in a situation of unheard-of bravery on a battlefield. But one thing she had never contemplated and that was taking any steps about herself. Magnificent futures came to girls like her. She believed from the bottom of her heart that lilies of the field should take no thought for the morrow. It was therefore only the way life should work out that Catherine was planning to send her to London.

"I'll like that," she said contentedly.

Pauline was used to her sister, but she did feel this was an occasion when she might have felt a bit anxious about what was going to happen to her.

"I can't think what they'll do with you," she pointed out. "You can't even sew as well as I can and goodness knows that isn't saying much. And you never could add. I suppose you must be able to add money to sell things. Mr. Bliss said he thought I'd sell."

"Is that the same boy who used to draw in his Bible in the sermon when we were little?"

Pauline suddenly remembered a fair untidy head bent over his Bible. He had sat across the aisle from them. She remembered the day when to their shocked delight he had turned the page round and shown them a crude caricature of the churchwarden, John Forbes, the same John Forbes at whose funeral the hat had appeared which reminded her of Petronella's.

"Yes."

Petronella looked at her.

"What are you thinking about? You've looked awfully queer since you came in. Sort of glazed. Did you eat too much tea?"

Pauline pulled herself together.

"It seems odd us going away. I've always supposed we'd always be here."

Petronella looked at herself in her pocket mirror.

"I haven't. People like this David Bliss were sure to turn up."

"He didn't turn up," said Pauline sharply. "Lady Bliss, asked him to have us out of kindness. It's awfully nice of him. We'll have to work terribly hard to make up."

Petronella put away her glass.

"There's nothing I could do in a dressmaking shop except

look nice, and that isn't hard work. What's David Bliss like now?"

Suddenly Pauline knew she didn't want to talk about David. She knew herself for a fool. Idiotic to go all silly about a man you had only just met. The sort of thing awful fools did in books. All the same, she couldn't bear to discuss him, however silly it was of her. There was something about him. The way he had of talking as if you were the only person in the world. Sudden confidential looks when the grown-ups were speaking that made you feel that you and he lived in a different world. And most binding of all, the way he held her elbow. Even now, thinking of it, she felt giddy.

"Just ordinary."

Petronella tried to look worldly.

"Of course there have not been a great many men in my life, but I think they're all different."

Pauline got up.

"There've never been any."

"No, not really," Petronella could skip from truth to fiction like a mountain goat. "But there'll be one when I meet David Bliss. That's a start."

Pauline stood still. She felt a quick frightened feeling go through her inside. It was the same feeling she got when she thought of eternity or thunder-storms hitting the house. Only those were silly things to think of because they might never happen, or at least when they did she would not be minding any more. But this fear was of something that had got to happen. Petronella must meet David. She couldn't keep him to herself.

Even as the fright went through her so did shame. She

never had been jealous of Petronella nor grudged her anything, and she didn't mean to start. She caught hold of her hand.

"Let's swear that whatever happens when we get to London we won't quarrel. Not over anything or anybody."

Petronella looked up at her in puzzlement.

"You are odd to-day. All right, I don't mind swearing. But I never quarrel, you know that."

Pauline looked at the sky. It was true. Petronella never quarrelled. She just took what she wanted.

"All the same let's swear it," she said. "I may need it if you don't."

Wives know that when they have to persuade their husbands into doing something, there are certain parts of the day which are best for tackling it.

Catherine tried very hard to persuade herself that it would be better to leave talking over plans with Mark until Monday morning. But she couldn't fool herself. After supper on Sunday was always Mark's relaxed time. It was then over his pipe he discussed next week's problems.

To-night was no exception. Supper over, he sank into an armchair by the window. Catherine noticed with a constricted heart that his suit was looking more green than black. That his new shoes were already getting that ridge across the toes. What a pity it was, she thought, that training colleges for clergy didn't teach the men how to pray without ruining their shoes. Prayers were just as good without your toes bent under you. She saw, too, how tired he was. It showed in the pause before he filled his pipe. Even that was an effort.

Petronella turned the wireless on. She played it very softly because it was something cheerful from abroad, and not the music selected by the B.B.C. for Sundays.

Catherine looked across at her.

"Darling, Daddy's tired. Why don't you and Pauline go and listen to the wireless in the schoolroom?"

"Oh, Mum," Petronella sighed, "I wish you weren't so B.B.C. minded. There's a lovely concert from Beecham's pills. I should think it would do Daddy good. After all, he's heard hymns all day, he can't want any more."

Mark smiled at her over his pipe.

"There are six days for that sort of music, Petronella. Can't you find a good classical concert for to-night?"

"Oh, very well," Petronella turned the switches. "It's a Bach cantata. I hope you'll enjoy it. They sound to me like a choir practice, only worse."

Catherine made the excuse of getting her embroidery to nudge Pauline. Pauline was sitting in a trance and had not heard a word of the conversation, but a nudge from her mother meant she was needed. She looked round inquiringly. Catherine jerked her head towards the door.

"Don't you think, Pauline, you'd rather hear Beecham's pills in the schoolroom?"

Pauline focused on the wireless. Petronella, to make the cantata worse, had turned it on at full blast. She grasped what was wanted of her. She got up and switched it off.

"Goodness, yes. Come on, Petronella."

Mark was relieved by the cessation of noise, but he liked to have his daughters about on Sunday nights.

"If it's a case of Beecham's pills or my daughters, I choose the pills."

33

Pauline came across and kissed him.

"It isn't, darling. We'll be back."

"I don't see why if Daddy doesn't mind — " said Petronella.

Pauline grabbed her arm.

"Come on, you fool."

Catherine threaded her needle with wool. She was covering six dining-room chairs in *petit point*. This was the second. The girls were supposed to be doing one each, but somehow they never got time. She looked down at the petal on which she was working. Should she allow herself to finish it before she started on Mark?

Mark turned his head towards her.

"I'm afraid Petronella hasn't a very critical musical taste."

Catherine took a stitch.

"She hasn't any taste, critical or otherwise. They haven't either of them much over anything. They can't have, living here."

Mark looked contentedly out into the garden. It was dark now, but a glorious smell of night-flowering stocks was drifting in.

"They're happy, and they're good. I wish we could give them more advantages, but we can't."

Catherine straightened her back and gripped her embroidery.

"We can and we're going to. I arranged it, to-day. Lady Bliss has found work for them both in London. They start to-morrow week."

Mark turned round and stared at her.

"Catherine! Without asking me? My dear, a step like that needs thought and prayer."

Catherine shook her head.

"No. Sending the girls to that boarding-school for the children of clergy needed thought and prayer, and you thought and prayed so long they were educated while you were doing it. Having them sent to someone for languages needed thought and prayer, and you're still thinking and praying, and they don't know a word of German and hardly any French. Sending them to stay with my family for two months needed thought and prayer and they've never been. But I don't need much thinking or praying to tell me they can't stop here all their days. They're seventeen, they must get away. They must meet people."

Mark's voice was stern.

"Why?"

Catherine dropped her embroidery. She got out of her chair and sat on the arm of his. She rubbed her face against his cheek.

"Because when I was their age I went away from home. I met a man just down from Oxford. If I hadn't gone away I should never have met him. And if I'd never met him I should have missed all the happiness I've had."

Mark picked up her fingers.

"Have I made you happy? Sometimes I think I get engrossed in my work and forget you. And, then, we're so poor."

Catherine smiled.

"I should hate you not to put your work first. And what on earth does being poor matter when a person has been as happy as you've made me."

"I don't see," said Mark, "that letting the twins work in London proves they'll meet men they can love. They're just as likely to meet them here."

Catherine gave him a slight shake.

"You're a silly goose, and a dreamer with your head in the clouds. There's never been a marriageable man in this village and I don't suppose there ever will be."

"But what work are they going to do? And where are they going to live?"

"Say first," Catherine ordered, "that you want them to have as fine a chance of happiness as we've had."

Mark smiled up at her.

"Heaven's best gift is a happy marriage. If I thought . . ."

"Now listen . . ." said Catherine.

Half an hour later the twins slipped into the garden. They peered in through the drawing-room window. Catherine was still on the arm of Mark's chair. He was still holding her hand.

"It looks all right," Pauline muttered.

"Aren't they soppy? " said Petronella.

Pauline stared at her parents. She spoke in a whisper.

"I expect if you're fond of someone it's rather nice."

Moira, like all competent people, liked to be left to run her own job in her own way. One of her jobs was engaging the staff. The staff at "Reboux" was complete to the last little "matching girl". It was, therefore, with natural irritation that she heard that the twins were coming.

"Mercy, what for? If your aunt must feel charitable about the dreary off-spring of vicarages, why not let her support them?"

"Oh, well," said David apologetically, for he quite saw Moira's point, "she's always been a saint to me."

"I dare say. But what on earth d'you think we're going to do with them?"

"I thought they might work in the show-room. Sell or something. Come on, my sweet. Don't look so sour. Come out to lunch in that new black and white and make every woman at the Berkeley swoon with envy."

Moira turned to go. Then a thought struck her. Was this philanthropy real or feigned?

"What are they like?"

David had spent quite a few odd moments since Sunday in trying to remember exactly what Pauline was like. His memory was of something very nice to have around, but Moira was one of those women before whom you certainly didn't praise another woman.

"Oh, I don't know. Just young."

"Are they alike?"

David had no intention of focusing Moira's eye on Pauline.

"Of course, they're twins."

Moira went away to change. She did not want two more girls, but, at least, they were evidently nothing to David. If they were, they'd go or she'd know the reason why.

The twins came to London on Saturday. Catherine took them up and stayed with them until Monday morning. In the ordinary way there was an early train on Monday mornings which would bring them back from their week-ends at the Vicarage, but this first week-end they had to have time to settle in.

Miss Williams had her club for girls in the Cromwell Road. At the first glance it was clear it was a most respectable place to live. There was a great deal of good solid carpet, and a great deal of very bright paint, and smells of cabbage and disinfectant. All those adjuncts, in fact, which make those who run clubs in London for "really nice" girls hope that they are providing such a home-like atmosphere that their girls will come dashing back every night, forgetting there are such things as latch-keys.

Miss Williams was so like David had described her that the twins had a terrible struggle not to laugh. Her teeth stuck out so far that she hissed when she talked. She had always been thin, but with the years she had grown so flat that except for which way round her head and feet were, she was the same either side. Never had a woman less curves. She had a brisk manner, and most of the girls put in her care loathed her, but the moment she set eyes on Petronella she oozed sweetness.

In the village at home it had been accepted with the years that Petronella was one over whom people cooed and one whom all wished to pet and pat. But Catherine had supposed (when she thought about it, which was not often) that this was because they had known her from childhood. On the journey to London it became distressingly clear that the wish to pat and pet was not going to be confined to Farlynge. The perfectly empty third-class carriage in which they had started, became frighteningly full. Men hurrying up the platform with eyes seeking empty corner seats suddenly saw instead Petronella. From that moment all thoughts of comfort and corners left them, and they crowded in, and having crowded in, surreptitiously, from behind their papers, they stared. And in every staring eye was the desire to pat and pet.

As usual, the sight of so much affection being bestowed on Petronella made Catherine practically burst with the need to bestow it on Pauline. She made herself a positive nuisance all the way to London by constant suggestions for Pauline's comfort.

"Would you like the window open, darling?"

"Would you like this picture paper?"

"Would you like some chocolate?"

Pauline, in a daze at the thought that it was now Saturday, and by the day after to-morrow she would see David every single day, never even noticed her mother's solicitude. Any more, indeed, than Petronella noticed the worship of the horribly over-crowded carriage. That was one of the things that was so difficult to combat in Petronella. If she noticed worship she never cared. Just swept it in as a right. Embarrassingly for Catherine, she paid no attention to the carriage full of young men, or rather accepted the whole lot as friends and carried on with her conversation exactly as if she were at home.

"Do you think I could have one of those bathing-dresses? They aren't a bit more expensive than any other."

She turned round the paper she was reading, not only to Catherine, but to the carriage at large. The picture showed a Hollywood bathing belle in trunks and a brassière.

"I think it would suit me."

Nobody answered. But the beating of the male hearts in the carriage was practically audible. There could be no question as to how she would look in such things, if anyone were lucky enough to see her.

"Do you suppose," she asked later, "that I've got sex appeal?"

Catherine longed to smack her. Longed to be able to feel the question was asked in a spirit of coquettishness that needed snubbing, but she could not. The question was asked in all innocence. Petronella was a fool. She was quite incapable of seeing even her own charms.

It was the same when they arrived at Victoria Station. People, of course, could not crowd into their taxi, but it was obvious that a lot of people would like to. Even the porter got sentimental. He insisted on carrying Petronella's film papers.

"You give those to me." He smiled at her.

"Carrying things makes you hot, don't they?"

Petronella smiled seraphically back and handed over her papers. Catherine looked at the large bunch of flowers and the book Pauline was clasping. She felt bitter.

"There's one thing," she comforted herself, "Miss Williams will treat them both alike, and so will the shop."

So it was with horror Catherine saw Miss Williams' change. From a brisk, efficient woman who would know what hour the twins got home every day, and who would see them safely off to catch their train on Saturday, she suddenly became all tender-hearted and solicitous. There was something worshipping in the way she looked at Petronella. Catherine could not know that a fourteen-year-old, much-loved Pekinese had just died and that the Williams' heart had an empty place that needed filling. That to her something so obviously pettable and spoilable as Petronella was a gift from heaven.

"I expect you like breakfast in bed, don't you?" she said to her.

Petronella stared at her with incredibly blue eyes almost

hidden behind her lashes.

"We never do unless we're ill."

"Well, just as a teeny extra treat sometimes," Miss Williams suggested, falling back naturally into Pekinese talk.

Petronella giggled. Catherine looked as severe as her face could manage. She spoke firmly.

"The girls have been very simply brought up. There is only one rule we insist upon. What one has, they both have."

"Really!" Miss Williams turned surprised eyes on Pauline.

"Yes, really," said Catherine. But even as she spoke she knew it would not happen. Pauline already had a roving eye round the bedroom. It was plain she was planning where everything could go. Petronella looked nowhere in particular. Why should she? If one thing was certain in life, it was that someone else would put the things away for her.

"Reboux" was in Bruton Street. Catherine saw the twins on to their proper bus. She told them where to get off. She stood on the corner and watched the bus career away up the Cromwell Road. It seemed so queer to be sending the twins off to work. It seemed only a few weeks since they were children. They were, of course, really children now. Only seventeen. But they had plainly reached the age when people stopped thinking of them as children. When, puzzled Catherine, retracing her steps to Miss Williams' club to collect her suit-case, did children stop being children? When did the moment come when men, instead of looking at your daughters as if they were sisters, looked at them with that very different look?

Pauline and Petronella got off the bus at Hyde Park Corner, as instructed. "It will give you a little walk, darlings," Catherine had said. Pauline was silent. Petronella carried on a monologue all the way. Pauline answered Petronella by "Ums", her mind on the fact that at last it was Monday.

In a quarter of an hour she would see him. Well, perhaps not quite in a quarter of an hour. Perhaps people who owned shops didn't come early. She did hope she would say the right thing. Somehow thinking of him so much made her terribly nervous. It would be awful if she couldn't answer and looked a fool.

Nine o'clock at "Reboux" was the hour when the entire staff poured in. Everybody hated Mondays. Nobody felt socially minded. Pauline and Petronella came inside with everybody else.

"Could you tell me, please . . ." Pauline said to a hurrying stranger.

"Who do you want? Which department?"

"I don't know," Pauline replied feebly, "just to sell, I think."

"I should wait."

Pauline looked at Petronella. Petronella needed no advice to wait. Here she was, where she was told to be. She had made sufficient effort for one day. When anyone wanted her they could fetch her. She had found a chair and somebody's picture paper. She was calmly reading.

"You can't do that," Pauline protested. "We're being paid to work."

Petronella yawned.

"Well, go and find someone."

"But they said we'd better wait."

Petronella stretched her legs.

"Well, aren't we? You know I can't think what you're in such a fuss about. You kept fussing we'd be late, and made me start before I'd eaten half enough breakfast. And now you're fussing because we aren't working."

"It's because we're new," Pauline explained. "I do think it would be awful if Mr. Bliss came in and found us just reading papers."

"Only me reading one." Petronella turned over a page. "You can just look busy. Oh, here's a picture of Claudette Colbert! I was thinking last night, I wonder if I'd look nice with a fringe."

A rather angry-looking, nervous, fidgety little woman came hurrying along the passage. She started talking before she reached them.

"Now, what are you two doing here? Who? What! Oh, yes. Mrs. Renton left orders about you. I'm Miss Jones, her secretary. Come along to my office. You're to wait until she comes."

"Mrs. Renton?" said Pauline. "I mean . . . at least, I thought we were to see Mr. Bliss."

"Now, come along, come along, come along," Miss Jones quacked fussily. "Mrs. Renton likes her orders to be obeyed. No, dear, of course you won't see Mr. Bliss. It's Mrs. Renton who handles the staff. Now, do come along. Mrs. Renton does not like the staff in the hall. This way."

Pauline followed her. She tried not to look miserable. But it was a blow. Not to see him at all! And he said himself he'd see her on Monday week. She heard a noise behind

her and looked round. Petronella was giggling. She had
stuffed her handkerchief in her mouth so that Miss Jones
would not hear.

"Whatever is it?" Pauline whispered.

Petronella took out the handkerchief. She spoke in a
gasp.

"Her. She's just like Donald Duck."

The twins were put to sit side by side in Miss Jones'
office. It was a bare little room with just a desk, a few
chairs and a typewriter. Miss Jones had stamped her
individuality on it by a bunch of sweet-peas in a vase on
the desk, and a coloured print from some Christmas annual
of Princess Elizabeth and Princess Margaret which was
framed and hung on the wall. The rest of the room was as
she had found it. Even Miss Jones' hat and coat were out of
sight. One could not help feeling that it would be very easy
to take an india-rubber and erase Miss Jones. She would
scarcely leave a mark.

Having disposed of the twins where she could watch
them, Miss Jones got down to the day's work of opening
and typing the letters. As long as she did this it was all
right, Petronella behaved herself. But sometimes the
telephone rang and then Miss Jones quacked down it in
funny pointless little rages.

"No, no, no, no. Mrs. Renton is not here. Please speak
slower. Yes, yes, yes. Of course I'll tell her."

The moment she began to speak Petronella began to
laugh. She laughed till the tears poured down her cheeks.
Pauline looked at her in horror. How awful of Petronella.
Didn't she care a bit that Mr. Bliss had made special jobs for
them when he didn't really want them?

It happened that day that Moira and David met on the doorstep. A house telephone rang sharply on Miss Jones' desk.

"Oh, is she? Yes, of course, I'm ready." Miss Jones turned to the twins. "Mrs. Renton's here." She looked in shocked surprise at Petronella. "Good gracious, child, why are you laughing? Mrs. Renton doesn't like that sort of thing at all."

David said in the showroom.

"Have some twins arrived?"

The girl questioned nodded.

"With Miss Jones."

"Right," he said.

Moira frowned.

"Really, David, there's no need for you to bother with them. I'll find them work."

"My dear aunt's protégées! Certainly I'll see them. Come on."

Moira and David came into Miss Jones' room. The twins were behind the door, so for a second they did not see them. Pauline, with a throb of happiness, saw David. She tried not to look pleased to see him but she did not succeed very well. David beamed at her.

"Hullo, Pauline, how's . . ."

He stopped. His mouth was not quite closed. There must come moments when beauty can wind you. Petronella's was the sort that winded easily. To David it seemed as though Miss Jones' drab little office were suddenly full of light. It was as if a bare back yard were full of flowering cherry.

Pauline watched his face. Something cold, like a pointed end of ice, stuck in her heart.

Moira was no fool. She never pretended to herself something was not there when it palpably was. Petronella's beauty was most assuredly flaming in front of her. And David, for some reason, had lied. She had said, "What are they like?" And he had answered, "Oh, I don't know, just young." And she had said, "Are they alike?" And he had answered, "Of course, they're twins." Alike! Was there ever such a lie? A feeling which must have been very familiar to Lucrezia Borgia swept over her. She looked imperious and a hard gleam shone in her eyes. That girl must go, she decided. No matter how I fix it. She's going.

Pauline looked up. She caught the expression on Moira's face. She read it quite rightly. She was startled. The look that woman had given Petronella was horrible. The look she had given David was possessive. She rose in that second above her own hurt. David might be staring like a blinded moth at Petronella. Well, why not? She had been a fool to let herself think of him so much. But one thing she was clear about. This strange, cruel-looking woman was not going to interfere.

Moira turned casually to Pauline to discuss work. She saw the expression on her face. She took a deep breath. So this girl was going to be tiresome. She'd teach her.

"I haven't really any work for you two," she said coldly. "But there are thousands of patterns downstairs. I want them sorted. You can go and start now."

David put his arm round Petronella.

"You don't have this twin. I'm going to design models on her."

Moira was far too clever to show any sign of annoyance. She merely nodded. She looked across at Miss Jones.

"Take Pauline down to that cupboard in the basement. Show her our indexing of patterns system."

It was not cleverness, but just courage that made Pauline show nothing. Petronella with David's arm round her. Petronella to have dresses designed on her. Not a word to herself. She was just sent down to the basement to sort patterns.

Moira watched her go with pleasure. She always enjoyed knowing other women were hurt.

CHAPTER 3

"REBOUX" WAS rushed. June was always busy, but this June was frightful. All the usual clothes, only more of them. The place swam with yards of brocade for Court gowns; it foamed with laces, chiffons and organdies for the Eton and Harrow, and for Ascot; the workroom looked like a rainbow with all the materials for evening dresses for this and that function which dripped off the tables; there was blue serge about the place, for Cowes was in sight; bales of the newest tweeds were arriving, for David was already designing for Scotland; and as for the weddings, even the workroom girls, who usually took a proud interest in their weddings, yawned at the sight of a bit of orange blossom. Into this whirlpool of labour the twins plunged, or rather, more accurately, Pauline plunged, and Petronella walked in at the shallow end.

To everybody else in the dressmaking world the model girls appear pampered pets. To them it seems that when not trying on or showing a dress they just lie and gossip in easy chairs. At "Reboux", in times of strain, they even had their strength kept up by mid-morning glasses of port. What the other departments said about those easy chairs and glasses of port was nobody's business.

The models themselves considered they had a hard life. They knew the weariness of standing for fittings. They knew that the moment they did settle in those easy chairs there would be a call: "Violet, show the green chiffon." "Mary, the white and pink *faille*." "Betty, the rust tweed." "Eloise, the initialled *tailleur*." They knew that no matter

48

how they might be feeling, the moment the call came, on had to go the clothes and into the showroom they had to glide, looking exquisite. Only a girl who has done it knows how it feels to have to look exquisite to order any time between nine and six.

The model girls were no more pleased to see Petronella than four girls who have worked together for a year are likely to be at having a newcomer shoved in amongst them. More especially as the room only comfortably held four lounge chairs and the fifth made a crowd. But Petronella had never known what it was like not to be wanted, and took it for granted they were pleased to see her. She could see at once that the models were just the sort of people she had always wanted to meet. There they lay in hardly any clothes (and those of satin), looking, she thought, like one of the better scenes in a picture.

"Oh!" she said admiringly, "how do you do? Do I take my clothes off, too? I hope not, for I haven't got those sort of underclothes."

The eyes of Violet, Mary, Betty and Eloise opened wide. Never in their lives had they seen anyone so lovely.

"Come in," said Violet.

Petronella came in, then with a gasp of pleasure she saw the walls. Pictures of practically every film star in the world, hanging in rows.

"Do you like film stars, too?" The models nodded. "Oh, I am glad. At home I never get a real chance to talk about them. My family are so silly. They never can remember them."

After that it was easy. If ever a girl fitted like a glove in with four other girls, it was Petronella. There were very few topics of conversation any of them could carry on with for long. Of these, film stars came first, followed by clothes, and if they would look better if they changed their hairdressing.

"Now I am glad," said Petronella, "you're interested in sensible things like hair. At home they say, 'It looks very nice as it is,' which isn't an answer at all."

"What do they talk about?" asked Eloise.

"You wouldn't believe how dull," Petronella explained. "Things like plants in gardens and books."

To Petronella nothing in life was really surprising because she had always known things would happen to her, but she really was enchanted to work at "Reboux". For a girl who all her life has wanted to try on clothes, to be paid to do it seemed like a miracle. To be expected to lie in between times gossiping with the sort of girls you have always wanted to know. And no trouble about anything. Everything given you to put on. Even the underclothes she wore.

"I'm designing and providing underclothes for my models," David explained to Moira. "Otherwise the little wretches will have bumps from suspenders and things ruining my frocks."

Shell pink satin brassières and panties he designed, which fitted like skin. He ordered stockings which held themselves up. He provided beige satin shoes.

The girls' sets of underthings were made in the workroom. Petronella, the first time she put on hers, knew that satin was one of her natural elements.

"Goodness," she sighed, kicking aside the garments of inexpensive flowered material which Catherine had provided. "Me for silk always. I've always thought I was that sort of person."

"You'll have to buy the ones you wear outside, then," said Betty. "Heaven help you if you're caught wearing these home."

"Well, I'm paid on Friday, aren't I? I'm to get three pounds a week. That awful Miss Williams where we live has one pound fifteen. That's for the room I share with Pauline and breakfast and dinner. Then my week-end ticket home costs six shillings. That leaves nineteen shillings for me. Could I buy satin or *crêpe de Chine* for that?"

"Can you sew?" asked Eloise.

"Well, I learnt. But I can't really. Not anything I could wear."

Eloise looked at Betty.

"She does want some clothes. She'd better sub on salary."

"How do I do that?"

Betty raised her hand and conducted the other three. They sang:

> "If you want a half-hour off,
> If you want a loansy,
> If you want to leave the room,
> You'll have to ask the Jonesy."

But Petronella believed in asking for things from people who were likely to give them to you. At least twice every day David sent for her. He was designing some autumn models on her. At least, that's what he was trying to do. But Petronella had the most devastating effect on him. When

51

she was in the room he really did not know if he was holding a length of taffeta or tweed. All his life he had loved beauty. The incredible perfection of Petronella absolutely fascinated him. He wanted her there all the time. Just to look at—to touch.

"I say," said Petronella, glancing over her shoulder at him as he knelt on the floor pinning some pleats, "do you think you could advance me some salary?"

He looked up at her smiling.

"What for, Peter?" (From the day they arrived, the twins were Peter and Paul to the shop.)

"Well, I think I've got used to satin underneath. I want to buy some."

She looked so delicious it was all David could do not to say, "Darling, go where you like, order what you like, and send me the bill." But he kept his head.

"All right. I'll tell the Jones to give you five pounds. She can take back ten shillings a week But stand still, duckie, or you'll get a pin in your tum."

Moira came back to her flat the evening of the twins' first day at "Reboux" in a filthy temper. Her maid, Ida, shuddered when she saw her face.

"I'll turn on your bath, Madam," she suggested hurriedly.

Moira nodded.

"And for heaven's sake see it's right. Don't tell me you thought it would be hot enough. Feel it and see it's hot enough. And put out the drinks. I'll have a whisky before I dress."

Ida turned on the bath. She poured in practically a box of

52

green powder. It was scented, and it foamed like the crests of small waves. She felt the water anxiously. Then turned off the taps. She opened Moira's bedroom door.

"Ready, Madam."

Moira, in a jade satin dressing-gown and mules, was sitting at her dressing-table. She scowled.

"All right, you fool, I can hear the water isn't running, can't I?"

Ida went into the sitting-room. She got out the whisky decanter and glasses. She rang the house telephone for a freshly iced siphon of soda. The waiter who brought it gave a look round.

"*She* in?"

"*She*," said Ida severely, "is the cat's mother."

The waiter put down the siphon.

"And about right too. Cat's mother describes her to a T, if you ask me. What's she like to-day?"

Ida gave up being grand. She needed a little sympathy.

"Awful. Just awful. Treats me like a dog."

The waiter went to the door. "I wonder you stay."

Ida gave a sly smile.

"Well, where you have her sort there's pickings."

The waiter winked.

"I'll say there are." He went off smiling down the passage.

Moira lay down in the bath. If there was one place in which she could think clearly, it was in her bath. There was something about hot, scented water which made her see things in focus. "And my goodness," she thought, waggling her toes to make the water foam, "things need a bit of thinking out."

53

She lay quite still and stared at the ceiling. It was a pleasant ceiling to stare at if you happened to fancy yourself, being entirely of glass. She thought back over the day. There had been that bad start with those maddening twins arriving. David behaving like a schoolboy over Peter. There had been that tiresome exchange of looks with Paul. That had annoyed her for hours. Something about Paul's exit had made her think that the wretched child had got the better of her. Then there was trouble the whole morning over fittings. Everybody changing their times and nothing ready. Every department blaming everybody else. When David had asked her to come out and lunch she had been just in the mood to settle down with a cocktail and some cold salmon and relax. It was then David had sprung the nastiest knock of an already hateful day. "Would you," he had said, "care to have a partnership?" Thinking of it now, relaxed in her bath, she could only admire the Moira who had heard the question at Claridge's at lunchtime.

"You kept your head, my girl," she told her reflection in the ceiling. "I'll have to hand you that."

For somehow miraculously she had the wit to say "No". It had not been easy, for in spite of her income, all she was paid, and the extra she acquired defrauding the accounts she still never made ends meet. Moira's ends were the sort that never would meet unless they were made of unbreakable elastic. The partnership she had in mind was marriage. Married to David all these old prudes would forgive and forget. Besides, married to David she intended to talk him into a joint banking account. Her eyes gleamed at the thought. A right to write cheques on David's account would be real money at last.

"No, thank you," she had said, apparently calmly eating her salmon.

"*No!*" David had looked startled. "Why not?

She had shrugged her shoulders.

"Well, it would tie me too much. I hate to be tied. I'm afraid of roots."

Without apparently looking at him, she had the satisfaction of seeing a flick of worry cross his face. He hadn't said any more. That wasn't his way. But she knew the conversation would come back and bother him. He wouldn't want to lose her. She was too useful. In the night watches he might begin thinking how to tie her up. The answer was obvious.

That was how she had thought sitting at Claridge's. That was how she had thought throughout a busy afternoon. Then at a quiet moment when Miss Jones had brought her tea a sudden gnawing fear got her.

Why had David suddenly suggested a business partnership? It had never been mooted before, the thought at the back of his mind had been marriage, she could swear to it. Then what had changed him? Surely not that nit-witted little beauty Peter. But somehow as the afternoon wore on the more the thought of Peter nagged. Now she came to think of it there had been less feeling that he was going to ask to marry her since that Sunday he had been to his aunt's and had seen the twins. Had he fallen for Peter then? Perhaps he had. Now she remembered that at luncheon at the Berkeley in the week after he had seen his aunt, she had told him something a little crude about her doings the night before. Usually he would have laughed. But that time he had suddenly stopped with his glass half-way to his lips, and an odd look in his eyes as if he were straining to see beauty through a dirty window. "Sordid, aren't you, my sweet?" he had said. "Have another cocktail."

Peter! That fluffy-brained little idiot. The more she thought of her the more she raged. The trying thing was she couldn't get rid of her, not yet anyway. Not while David stared at her as though he were blinded.

"Now," she asked the reflection on the roof, "what next?" The water lapped pleasantly and scentedly against her. She looked thoughtful. Then suddenly a smile turned the corners of her mouth. She sat up. "That's it, of course, Paul!" She picked up the soap and began to wash. "I must find something that will break her. Something which will make her decide when she goes home next weekend that she'd like to stop there."

It was at that moment that she had her bright idea. "Reboux" worked on four floors. There was the top floor where the sewing was done. The second was the stockrooms, dispatch department, models' room, and Miss Jones' office. The ground floor had the showroom, David's room and her room. In the basement were more cupboards, and the staff kitchen, looked after by Mrs. Brown, who was also the cleaner. At all times and particularly when there was a rush, somebody had to be spared from different floors to take messages to someone. In future Pauline could be messenger. She could be runner for everybody. If that didn't kill her, nothing would. If she knew her heads of staff, the moment they had a runner they would find something for her to run for, if for no better reason than that they had as much right to her as anybody else. Moira smiled happily. She soaped vigorously. She had no right to do it. A runner was hardly the job David had in mind for his aunt's protégée. But he probably wouldn't notice. He was so engrossed by the other twin he wouldn't bother what happened to Paul. Moira carefully soaped her neck.

"One week of that ought to see her through. And with any luck if she goes they'll both go." She leant over for her sponge. "And if that doesn't work I've another think coming."

Pauline had a wretched first day at "Reboux". She, the friendliest of people, to be shut up in the basement sorting patterns. The indexing Miss Jones had shown her was not difficult. It did not take her many minutes to grasp it; what made her a bit slow was herself. Every now and again she would stop and think of Petronella upstairs with David's arm round her. She couldn't, she wouldn't, she told herself, be jealous. That was hateful. Besides, she had made a swear not to quarrel.

"But, oh, goodness," she thought, sitting on the floor with her lap full of patterns and a tear dripping off her nose, "I don't want to grudge her looking like she does, but I do wish, since there were two of us being born at once, that God had fussed a bit more about me."

It was at one of these moments that Mrs. Brown had found her.

Mrs. Brown held a position of honour at "Reboux". Her husband, after a perilous career, had become boot-cleaner and odd-job man at the house where David lived while he coached for the diplomatic. For David he had the greatest respect, as he had backed him successfully when he rode in a point-to-point. When David left off coaching and went to Paris, naturally he saw no more of the Browns. But one day, when he was back in London superintending the decorating of his shop, he was told someone was outside waiting to see him. There he found Mrs. Brown, her face puffed with tears.

"Oh, sir," she wailed, "Brown's got into trouble again. Over a safe it was. He's in for ten years. He says to come to you. A gentleman who can ride an old screw same as he did and make him win won't let anybody down, he says."

David patted her arm.

"That horse wasn't a screw." Then he thought a moment. "I'll want someone to clean here, and to keep the kitchen in order for the girls. How's that?"

"That," said Mrs. Brown, "would be fine." Then she added, "You're a gentleman, sir."

Her position at "Reboux", however, was not only based on David's patronage. It was based on real affection.

"I don't half like my girls," Mrs. Brown would say.

And the answer would have been:

"And your girls don't half like you."

Naturally all gossip filtered through to Mrs. Brown. The fact that twins had arrived called Peter and Paul had not missed her. She was in fact what she called "in a rare twitter" to see Peter, preferring to judge for herself if the stories of her beauty had been exaggerated or not.

Mrs. Brown was a very fat woman, but not so fat but that she could get down on the floor if necessary beside somebody who needed a bit of sympathy.

"There," she said, hugging Pauline to her, "there, my pet, what is it?"

Pauline, of course, did not tell Mrs. Brown what it was that had upset her. She pretended it was being lonely and strange on a first day. Mrs. Brown snorted.

"And no wonder. *She* would send you down here. When we first started, dearie, we didn't keep no Honourable trollops a-callin' of theirselves manageresses, and if you asks me we did a lot better without." She got up. "I'll make you a nice cupper tea. Nothing like it when you have the droops."

Over a cup of tea Mrs. Brown told Pauline all about the staff at "Reboux". Miss Blane, head of the workroom. "Looks sour, dear, but she has the indigestion something chronic. I'd act up once in a way meself if I 'ad the pain she 'as." Miss Maud, the second in the workroom. "Nice girl. Engaged to a nice boy. Doesn't half have a time with Miss Blane on a bad day." Pauline told her she had met Miss Jones. "Funny little half-worth," she said. "But I'm sorry for her. Got a mother in a loony-bin. Goes down every Sunday to see her. Has to pay a pound a week to keep her there too. Terrible drag on her it is. In the showroom there's Miss Edwards. She's all right, but scared of her own voice. She was going to get married only her boy lost his job. He's never had another. It's bad luck. He won't marry and live on her, and she's not gettin' any younger." She got up. "Well, I must see to me kitchen, I suppose." She patted Pauline's shoulder. "Don't fret no more. They can't always keep you down 'ere. Things'll look a tidy sight better to-morrow."

Things certainly were better in the morning. Pauline had scarcely arrived at "Reboux" when she heard Miss Jones wanted her.

"Now look here, dear," said Miss Jones. "Mrs. Renton has just telephoned. She wishes you to be messenger between the floors. Of course it's a busy season. We can't all do the work we'd like, you must just wait—"

"Oh, but — " Pauline interrupted, her eyes shining. "I do like. I think it's very kind of Mrs. Renton to think of it."

Miss Jones looked up sharply. Was this new girl daring to be impertinent? Mrs. Renton never was kind. And expecting a girl who was engaged to sell to run messages all day long would certainly not be a way of showing it.

"You don't understand, child," she snapped. For one glance at Pauline's face had convinced her the child really was pleased. "You are to run messages for all of us."

Pauline smiled happily.

"But of course I understand. You'll send for me, and so will the workroom and the showroom." She saw Miss Jones still did not believe she would be pleased. "It's a lovely job for me. You see, ever since I was little it's what I've done. Run to people with messages from Father. That's why I'm here really. Mum was afraid I'd become an extra curate always. Spinsters do sometimes, you know."

Miss Jones knew only too well lots of things spinsters could become. You could become a slave to a mother in an asylum who might live for years, draining your income, draining your strength as you spent your free time listening to her mouthings. You could become a slave to a person you despised, like Moira, and yet go on being her slave because the work was secure and you didn't dare be out for a week, because of Mother. Her eyes blinked behind their glasses. What did this child know, she secure in her vicarage?

60

"Now don't stand there smiling. Run away, child, run away."

Pauline was quite unmoved by her tone. "She sounds cross," she thought, "but I expect it's worry. It must be awful to have a mother like hers."

"I expect I seem terribly slow," she explained cheerfully. "But honestly I won't be when I'm a messenger. Just tell me where I'm to wait when I'm not wanted, and how I'm to know when I am."

"If you'd not be so impatient I was coming to that. You'll wait in the basement. There's a bell there rings for Mrs. Brown. When it rings twice it'll be for you. Mrs. Brown will show you where the indicator is so that you know which floor wants you."

Pauline turned to go. Then she looked back over her shoulder.

"Please thank Mrs. Renton. Tell her she couldn't have found anything I'd like better."

Miss Jones sat looking at the door which had shut behind Pauline. For a moment the angry expression faded from her face. Then with an annoyed jerk of her shoulders she went on with her work. "It's not my business," she thought. "Besides, we go through it, why shouldn't she?"

Pauline positively skipped down to the basement. If ever a person was in luck she was. No awful sitting sewing. No trying to sell when you were sure to make a fool of yourself. Just running messages, a thing she'd always done. And to be paid for it! Besides, it would mean she would see David sometimes. It would be a funny thing if she never met him on any floor of his own shop.

"Oh, Mrs. Brown," she exclaimed, running to the

61

kitchen. "You were quite right. Things are much better this morning. I'm to be messenger for all the floors. I'm to sit down here with you, and when your bell rings twice it's for me. And will you please show me the indicator?"

A bell gave two sharp rings. Mrs. Brown took her hands from her sink. She led the way to the indicator in the passage.

"That's workroom." She dried her hands on her apron. "I'll lay odds there won't be much sittin' downstairs with me."

The twins were undressing.

"Fancy," said Pauline, "us going home to-morrow. I feel we've been in London years and years. Goodness!" She stared at Petronella. "Wherever did you get those?"

Petronella looked happily down at her apricot-coloured panties.

"I bought them. I've got three sets." She undid a parcel. "Look."

Pauline sighed.

"We are getting Londoners. Imagine us wearing satin."

"Well, you aren't," Petronella pointed out. "But you can borrow mine if you want to buy a dress or anything and what you've got underneath matters."

Pauline fingered the things fascinated.

"Where did you get the money?" She looked up startled. "You didn't spend all you got this week, did you? Because there's Miss Williams to pay and our tickets."

Petronella explained about the five pounds.

"And Mr. Bliss didn't mind a bit. He was awfully nice."

"Mr. Bliss!" Pauline carefully refolded the green satin set.

"Did you ask him?"

Petronella studied herself in the long glass.

"I really see him more than anybody."

"Do you?" Pauline managed not to sound envious. "Do you like him?"

"Um." Petronella turned round to get another view of herself. "We all do in the models' room. We think he looks like Clark Gable."

"Does he talk to you about things?"

"Um."

"What sort?"

"Oh, clothes; and asks about me. You know how people do. If I'm happy, and like working for him, and those sort of things."

"Does he ever talk about himself? I mean when he was little?"

Petronella came and sat on the end of her bed.

"I should hope he didn't. It's awful being fitted without that. He's designing a dress for me to show. It's for the evening. It's all made of tulle. All different colours. He spends hours and hours pinning bits on me. I look like a film star in it. I asked Mr. Bliss which one I looked like and he said, 'None, thank God,' and I said, 'Don't you like films?' And he said, 'Do they matter all that much?' And I said, 'Well, I'd rather look like a film star than anything else. Anybody would.' And he said, Had I ever been to the theatre? So I told him we'd seen 'Peter Pan' and the circus, and he laughed and said, 'We'll have fun. You and the other twin must come to the theatre one night'."

Pauline sat up.

"Both of us?"

63

" 'Course." Petronella finished undressing. "Why, not? We both work there."

Pauline got into bed. She lay very still stretched out under the sheets. Here was something she had not thought of. David wanted to be with Petronella, but being kind he would ask them both. He mustn't have to do that. Being twins people got in the way of asking them together. But now that they were grown up it was different. That David was fond of Petronella was the talk of the shop. "Never seen nothing like it," Mrs. Brown had said. "Knocked all endways he seems." Well, if that was how he felt he'd better have a chance to see Petronella. Nobody could say she was knocked all endways. She was knocked nowhere at all. She never was.

"I think," said Petronella, "I'll let Miss Williams see these." She nodded at her new things.

Pauline raised her head from her pillow.

"Why, do you want her to wash them?"

"I expect she'll have to." Petronella went to the door. "I've only three lots."

Pauline settled down again. She pictured Petronella in masses of tulle with David trying different shades on her. She wasn't envious. She had her own dreams of herself and David, and they had nothing to do with evening dresses. They were country dreams. Just talking by a river, and when he said, " I'm glad you're coming to work for me." Well, it hadn't happened that way. He hardly knew she was in the shop except that she was Petronella's sister. "Oh, well," she thought, turning over. "You've work you like and you do see him sometimes. That's something."

Petronella came in giggling.

"She wants me to call her Aunty-mum. She said the Pekinese did. She looked at these and she said, 'Oo's got lovely 'ittle things for Aunty-mum to wash'?"

"Poor fool," said Pauline.

Petronella yawned.

"She's bats. But I don't mind her thinking I'm her dog if she'll wash and iron for me!"

CHAPTER 4

THE DAYS went slipping by. The rushed hours at "Reboux". The gossipy evening meal at Miss Williams'. The quiet Saturday afternoons and Sundays at home when they were suddenly conscious that they were tired, and that food at home was a hundred times nicer than food in London.

To Moira's amazement, Pauline showed no sign of giving notice.

"How's that girl Paul getting on?" she asked Miss Jones hopefully on the Monday morning after the twins' first week-end at home.

"Admirably."

"Has she grumbled at all about the work?"

"No," said Miss Jones; and then added with relish, "She likes it."

"Likes it!" Moira turned away; there was something in Miss Jones' voice that made her feel that she suspected she had made an unpleasant job on purpose. "Well, that's good."

Miss Jones knew that Moira did not think it good. She was surprised to hear herself say:

"She's a very nice girl."

Moira certainly wasn't going to stand for that. She turned round blazing.

"My dear good creature, why should you bore me with your opinions of the staff? If I want them I'll ask for them."

Miss Jones cringed and looked apologetic, but deep inside

her she felt pleased. She was glad she had said what she had.

Moira spent quite a lot of her time puzzling over Pauline. She could not believe that anybody really liked running up and down stairs at the beck and call of any Tom, Dick and Harry in the place. She must be putting on an act. But why? Was she sticking around because of her sister? Moira had never got over Pauline's "touch-Petronella-if-you-dare " look that she had seen that first morning. Heavens, if she had a sister who looked like Petronella, anybody could kick her if they liked. The only share she would take would be urging them on. It must be vile having a sister prettier than yourself. But a twin who was a dyed-in-the-wool beauty must be torture. She kept harking back in her mind to her first instinct. She had been sure then that Pauline was a bit interested in David herself. Silly little fool if she were. David never even knew she was in the building.

It was not till almost the end of June that Pauline ran into David. She had seen him about, of course. Sitting at his desk with sketches strewn all over the floor. Standing in his doorway watching the models show frocks. Twice she saw him draping material on Petronella. Several times she saw him talking to her. Then on a Wednesday she crashed into him on the stairs.

It had been an appallingly busy day. There had scarcely been time for her to get down to the basement before her bell rang. The bride for a big wedding the next week, and all her bridesmaids (and there were twelve of them), were coming for final fittings the next day. The bell had been rung by Miss Edwards in the showroom.

"Oh, Paul dear, would you just slip up to Miss Blane and

ask her if she could spare one of the Manton bridesmaid dresses? Mrs. Renton has the florist here. She wants to see one against the flowers for effect." Then she lowered her voice. "If you can, dear, bring it down with you. You know how *she* hates to be kept waiting."

Pauline galloped up the stairs. Evidently Moira was on one of her rampages. It was a shame. As if poor Miss Edwards hadn't got enough to put up with anyway. It must be awful always seeing wedding dresses about when you so dreadfully wanted to get married yourself.

Miss Blane clearly had bad indigestion. Pauline knew the signs by now. A very pink tip to her nose and the rest of her face yellow. She approached her cautiously.

"Good morning, Miss Blane."

Miss Blane looked round.

"Good morning, Paul. If Miss Edwards has sent for any of the clothes for the Manton wedding tell her she'll be lucky if she can see one frock finished by late afternoon."

All the work girls stitched hard, their eyes never leaving their sewing. Pauline could see under the table from where she stood. She could see everybody nudging their neighbour with their foot. Each foot plainly said, "Hark at her!"

Miss Maud gave her a look. Pauline gathered that Miss Maud couldn't help. She smiled at Miss Blane.

"All right, I'll tell her. It was just one for a few minutes. There is a florist with Mrs. Renton. They want to try some flowers. I'm sure Mrs. Renton never meant a finished dress. She'd know one couldn't be. You're so rushed."

Miss Blane looked mollified. She was a brilliant fitter, and was afraid of no one, not even Moira. And of course if everybody knew downstairs how rushed they were, it made things feel better.

"Well, if you take them down yourself, Paul, and bring them back right away, I might manage to spare a couple." She looked along the work-table. "Connie, you let me have Lady Gloria's; you can get on with those bows on the train while it's gone. And, Miss Maud, you might get one of the little train-bearer's frocks out of the cupboard." She turned back to Paul. "That's just like Miss Edwards. She's forgotten, I suppose, that the children wear quite a different colour. How they ever sell anything downstairs, I can't think. They never use their brains."

Once more Pauline watched the demure-looking work-girls give each other a kick. She nearly laughed, but instead she managed to say:

"I'm afraid that's me. I think Miss Edwards did ask for one of the children's too."

Miss Blane's face softened.

"No wonder if you forget something now and again. The way that showroom keeps you running around."

Pauline didn't dare look under the table. She knew the girls must be signalling with their feet. No bell rang as often and as furiously as the workroom's, and of course they knew it.

Miss Maud came back with the little frock. Miss Blane picked up Lady Gloria's. She followed Pauline outside. Pauline looked at her sympathetically.

"Is your indigestion bad?"

Miss Blane handed her the frocks.

"Terrible. Stabbing pains round my heart. I don't know how to stand up sometimes."

"I'm so sorry. I do hope the stuff old Mrs. Brooks grows at home will do you good. I saw her on Sunday, but she says the seeds don't ripen till October. I'm afraid it'll be November before she's made it for you."

Miss Blane smiled grimly.

"I'll try anything, dear. But I've no faith in one of them. The bottles I took last year would have stocked a hospital."

Pauline hurried down to the showroom, Lady Gloria's green satin with its blue belt over one arm, and the child bridesmaid's buttercup yellow over the other. She handed them to Miss Edwards.

"Be as quick as you can with Lady Gloria's—it isn't done, and Miss Blane's got one of her bad turns."

Miss Edwards made an expressively understanding face.

"I'll do what I can." She hurried off towards Moira's office. "But you know what *she* is."

Pauline started towards the basement, when she heard a whistle from overhead. She looked up.

Mary was beckoning from the models' room.

"Be a sweet, Paul, and get us four ice-creams."

Pauline went upstairs.

"I daren't. My bell's sure to ring if I go out."

"It won't take you five minutes."

Pauline looked round the room.

"Where's Petronella?"

Violet glanced up from a paper she was reading.

"Gone to be photographed. *He's* taken her again. Very keen on how the photographs look, all of a sudden."

"Oh, well," said Betty, who was hurrying into a tweed suit. "It's a good thing really. He knows just how he wants his clothes posed."

70

Eloise was stretched out in her chair. She had not bothered with her dressing-gown, she just lay in brassière and panties.

"As soon as the rush dies down we've got to teach her to model. Then she'll know what work is, the poor girl. I've shown four frocks to that awful Miss Phipps this morning. She looks dreadful in anything anyway. And in about ten minutes there's that horrible Lady Fern coming with that fat daughter. I always have to show to them because she says I'm like the daughter. If that isn't a nerve I don't know what is. So you see, Paul dear, why I have to have an ice."

Paul held out her hand.

"Well, give me the money and I'll try. But I can't promise."

Clinking the money for four choc ice bars in her hand, Pauline went down to the basement. She could hear her bell ringing before she got to the top of the stairs.

Mrs. Brown looked out of the kitchen.

"That's rung twice, dear. It's Miss Jones. You'd better hurry."

Pauline put the money in her pocket.

"Thank you, Brownsy."

Miss Jones looked up at her over her glasses.

"Where have you been, child, where have you been? I've rung twice. Will you please go up to Miss Blane and tell her Mrs. Faucett-Eagles is leaving for Capri on Friday instead of next week. So will she see that all her things are round by twelve o'clock on Thursday morning."

Pauline looked at Miss Jones in despair.

"Goodness! With the Manton wedding all being fitted to-morrow. I bet she can't do it."

Miss Jones sniffed.

"She shouldn't get so behind. Always rush, rush at the last minute. Then we all have to suffer. I think it's very tiresome about Mrs. Faucett-Eagles. But she's a good customer. We can't fail her. The clothes were going on Saturday anyway."

"Yes, I know," Pauline agreed. She gave Miss Jones a grin. "Aren't you glad it's me that's telling Miss Blane and not you?"

Miss Jones looked cross.

"Really, child. Run along, run along." Then she gave Pauline a nod. "I know. It is trying for you. Why don't you tell Miss Maud? She can tell Miss Blane."

Up went Pauline's head.

"Goodness, no! I'm the runner here. I'll do my own dirty work."

Pauline went down to the showroom. Edwards was busy with a customer. Pauline quietly over and stood beside her.

Betty was showing the tweed suit. She twisted round in front of the customer with an aloof, expressionless face. As she faced Pauline she winked.

"It is a very nice line," said Miss Edwards. "Mr. Bliss will be all long revers this autumn. Turn round, Betty. You see the pockets. Very new, aren't they?"

The customer beckoned Betty to her so that she could examine the pockets. Pauline sidled up to Miss Edwards.

"Could I have Lady Gloria's frock? I've got an awful message to take to the workroom. It might help if I brought the frock back."

Miss Edwards made a slight nod towards Moira's door.

"*She's* still got it. I daren't go in."

72

Miss Blane had been angrier even than Pauline had thought she would be about the clothes.

"Go down," she said, "and see Mrs. Renton. Tell her it's impossible and ask her if we can send some of the things on to Capri."

It was no good arguing. Very depressed, Pauline went downstairs. "*Her,*" she thought. "Nobody's made me see *her* before."

Moira had just finished with the florist. Seeing florists was the sort of job she hated. That David, who should be seeing him, was out with Petronella, added to her wrath. The wretched Manton family. How like them to go to a good designer like David for the dresses and then try and ruin them all by making the bridesmaids carry delphiniums. As if David hadn't told them that the blue belts must be the only blue in the colour scheme. She had just lit a cigarette when Pauline tapped on her door.

"Come in." She glanced at Pauline. Then swung round to face her. "So she is going to give notice," she thought.

Pauline tried to like everybody. Her father had often told her that everybody had things about them to like if you looked for them. But Pauline hadn't had a chance to do any looking at Moira. She hadn't seen her since the first day she came to the shop, and that day (although she was afraid it was unchristian of her) she had quite definitely disliked her. She was determined not to feel anything about her now. Not to remember what Lady Bliss had said, or what she herself had felt. She was just an employee with a message to the manageress. She came to the desk. She gave the message.

Moira tapped some ash off her cigarette.

"Miss Blane should have come and seen me herself. I never discuss the policy of the business except with the heads of the departments."

"It's the Manton fittings to-morrow," Pauline reminded her. "Miss Blane's awfully rushed."

"We're all busy. Miss Blane no more than anybody else. Tell her I think it was an impertinence sending you. If she wants to ask anything she can come and ask me herself."

Pauline was angry.

"If anybody's impertinent, I think it's Mrs. Faucett-Eagles. Suddenly asking for her clothes early. Trying to pretend she doesn't know that it means that lots of the workroom girls will have to stay late."

Moira gasped. Never since she had been manageress had one of the staff dared to speak like that. Her tone would have hurt even an unsensitive person. It absolutely shrivelled Pauline

"Get out, and stay out. If you ever dare speak like that again, you go."

Pauline sat on the top step of the stairs leading to the basement. Much to her shame, she cried. She scolded herself for being so idiotic. " Goodness," she sniffed, "you that's seventeen, almost eighteen, crying like a baby. And you deserved what she said. It's not your business to talk like that. It's just because you were brought up in a vicarage, and everybody in the parish is nice, that you think you can say anything you like. All the same, she needn't have been quite so beastly. She's made me feel such a worm."

Her bell clanged. She gave her eyes a hurried rub and went down to the indicator.

It was the showroom. This time she was in luck, it was only Miss Edwards returning Lady Gloria's frock. She hung it over her arm and went up to Miss Blane.

Pauline's efforts to rub the traces of tears off her cheeks had not been very effective. As she opened the workroom door everybody looked up. The work-girls nudged each other.

"What a shame!"

"Fancy sending her down with a message like that."

"Bet *she* was awful. I'd rather take a message to a cage of tigers myself."

Miss Blane, too, looked at Pauline and was filled with remorse. She hurried across and took the dress from her.

"I gave Mrs. Renton your message." Pauline looked at the floor. "She wasn't very pleased at you sending me. She said she only discussed the policy of the business with the heads of departments. She said — "

"Yes?" inquired Miss Blane. "Go on, dear."

"Would you please go and see her yourself?"

This end was so obviously a fabrication that all the girls laughed. Pauline looked up.

"It was almost that, only not so polite. She said it was an impertinence sending me, and I said the impertinence was Mrs. Faucett-Eagles' not thinking of people having to work so late." All the eyes in the room were turned on her, horrified. "Yes, I know. I don't wonder you look like that. It's awful the way I just think things and then say them."

Miss Blane straightened her hair in front of the glass.

"Take charge, please, Miss Maud. I'm going down to have a talk with Mrs. Renton. Girls, get on with your work."

On the stairs Miss Blane turned to Pauline.

"I'm sorry I sent you. I won't again. But you had no right to say a thing like that. It's not your place."

"I know," Pauline agreed humbly. "But I've only just got a place. I never seem to have had one before. That's why I forget about keeping it."

As she went down to the basement she remembered the ices for the models. She went to Mrs. Brown.

"The models want ices. Miss Blane's with Mrs. Renton. If Miss Jones or Miss Edwards ring, be a lamb and say I've gone out on a message and won't be a minute."

"All right." Mrs. Brown went on cleaning the stove. "But what you want to run your legs off for those girls for, I don't know."

The cheerfulness of the street, and the nice casual air of the mews where she went for the ices, sent Pauline's spirits up again. She bought the bars for the girls and one for herself. She took a quick bite at hers while she was in the mews, well out of sight of "Reboux's" windows. She would have bought one for Mrs. Brown, but she knew she never ate ices because of her teeth.

Either the breath of air or the ice-cream did her good, for the morning seemed easier after that. She was just as rushed, only somehow nothing seemed as tiresome. There was a lot of fuss about sheets that Mrs. Brown had to put down in the morning for the Manton wedding. Mrs. Brown said the particular ones wanted were at the wash, and if people wanted things special they should say so. But that got settled in the end. Then there was a very awkward time spent running between the showroom, the workroom and the second floor, where the dispatching and packing were done, trying to trace a dress that should have been delivered the day before and hadn't been. The customer had come about it herself and was waiting in the showroom with a face stiff with rage. It was discovered at last that it had been sent to the wrong number. Pauline felt her respect for Miss Edwards soar as she heard her handling the situation. "Thank goodness they didn't make me sell," she thought. "I'd never have been able to do that. I'd have been sure to think, 'What a fuss! Why didn't she wear something else at her party'!"

The original idea had been that the twins should go out to lunch together. This quickly came to an end, as lunch was expensive. Besides, the models never went out unless they had a date. They had fearful meals in their own room of such things as sardines and cream buns.

Pauline had her meals in the basement. Lots of the girls came down and put things in the oven to warm, or made Bovril, tea or cocoa. She liked it. She liked talking to them all. She was tremendously interested in what they did. Eating her boiled eggs or ham sandwich, she would be absorbed in a discussion of what Cora had better wear when she went to meet her boy's mother. Or what Fanny had better do to get rid of her spots.

"Goodness," she would sigh as she put away her plate and cup, "they are nice, Brownsy."

Mrs. Brown would nod.

"As nice a lot in the workroom here as you'd find anywhere."

Sometimes there would be a minute or two after the girls had gone before her bell rang. Then Mrs. Brown would read Pauline's future in her tea-cup.

"You make a lovely marriage, dear. But that's what my

77

cup said before I married Brown, and look how that's turned out."

Often they would spend the time discussing Brown. And what he had last said when Mrs. Brown had been to see him in "The Scrubs".

To-day her bell began to ring almost before she had finished eating.

"They'll be surprised when your legs drop off," said Mrs. Brown.

It was nearly closing-time when she met David. She had been on a message for Miss Edwards about buttons. Just as she left the showroom he came along the passage.

"Hullo, Twin." He took hold of her arm. "I'll be seeing you on Sunday. I told Peter to ask your mother if I might come to tea. I'm playing cricket down your way, and staying with my respected aunt."

He had finished all he had to say. His impulse was to move on, and yet he stayed a moment. Pauline, hot, her hair a little untidy, somehow brought a whole lot of things into his shop which didn't belong. The river lip-lapping round stones. The smell of very young bracken. The sound of his horse's hooves on the gravel as she was led round from the stables. Sounds and smells that he had once heard and smelt until he grew up and forgot what noses and ears are for. That was the other twin. Odd he had forgotten all about her. The twin who had told him his suit was too good to lie about in. Who had been angry because when he was a small boy his mother had dared to marry again.

He gave the arm he held a friendly squeeze.

"See you Sunday." He went into his office and shut the door. Pauline stood a moment looking at the shut door.

Then she sighed. It was as if in letting that sigh go she let her happiness go too. It had been lovely while it lasted, that little talk, the way he had held her arm, but it meant nothing to him, she knew that. Just as she knew why he was coming to tea on Sunday. Why he had arranged to play cricket in their neighbourhood. But just for the seconds he had been there talking to her she had been incapable of thought, capable only of feeling. A saying she had heard in the nursery came back to her — "If wishes were horses." "If wishes were horses," she thought, "I'd get on mine and ride beside him always. If he didn't see me it wouldn't matter. I'd be there."

She gave herself a jerk. "Goodness," she thought, "look at me mooning outside his door. Lucky nobody saw."

But Moira had seen. Her office door had been ajar. She had heard what David had said. Afterwards she had opened the door wider and had seen Pauline too absorbed to notice things like opening doors. She had meant (simply as a means of working off her temper) to come out and flay Pauline. Any excuse would do. Hanging about the passage, anything as long as she had her to curse. But looking at Pauline she changed her mind "Poor, silly little fool," she thought. "Where does she think she comes in the picture? She must know about her sister. The entire shop talks of nothing else, blast their souls. If she knows, why doesn't she put up some fight to get hold of him? What appalling technique! Fancy saying to a man you were fond of 'That'll be lovely', in that tone of voice. What a give-away! David must think her a comic. It must have its funny side being adored by one twin while you made a fool of yourself over the other."

She came back to her desk and sat down. "Over the other!" My God, this going down to play cricket didn't look too good. Nor did this staying with his aunt. What more certain way to fix the aunt's eyes, and Peter's parents' eyes, on his infatuation, than to go there for the week-end. Was that what he wanted to do? Could he really be serious? A spasm of fear gripped her. It laid clammy fingers on the pit of her stomach. It couldn't be true. It mustn't be true. Peter was a kid. With her looks there would be thousands of men for her. For herself there was only David.

"I must get her out of here." Unconsciously she spoke out loud. "If he doesn't see her or the sister he'll get over it." She lit a cigarette. Her eyes stared into space. She felt marvellously alert. That at least the wretched Peter had done for her. The friction of her presence, and the knowledge that David was seeing her was a permanent excitement creator. Rage was as good a titillator of the senses as any drink or drug.

She had been smoking about five minutes when she grew taut. Anyone who knew her would have said, "Look at Moira, she's got an idea." Her eyes began to focus things in the room. The hand that was not holding the cigarette tapped nervously on the table. Then suddenly she relaxed.

"Slow, dear," she said to herself. "But damned clever. And practically bound to work. I'll start in on Monday."

CHAPTER 5

TEA WAS LAID on the lawn.

"Thank goodness," said Catherine, "I didn't pick all the roses. I nearly did, for there was a Women's Institute show on Friday over at Coombe House. Our Institute was showing collections of things. You know—jams and cakes and needlework and vegetables. Then suddenly Miss Green remembered that we'd said we'd show roses. Miss Green is a well-meaning secretary, but she is a fool. So very unwillingly I said I'd show some. I even began tacking black velvet over a box. Then luckily Mrs. Carter said she'd like to. She has some awful great things like cabbages. They didn't get commended, of course, but we did very badly anyhow, so that didn't matter."

Pauline rolled over and sniffed at a perfect orange bud.

"Fancy Lady Bliss coming to tea and you with no roses to crow about."

Catherine looked down at Pauline. Her voice was listless.

"I do hope London isn't being too much for you, darling. Even Daddy said he thought you looked a little pale, and you know how one has to look before he notices anything."

Pauline sat up.

"Of course it isn't. I feel perfectly well. It's just not getting as much air as usual. I'll get used to it."

"Where's Petronella?"

"Will you buy a tell?" Catherine nodded. "She said to get you to buy it before she came down. She's got on a new frock."

"Has she? Is it nice?"

Pauline swallowed. It was so nice that she had been startled. It had made her own appearance more "the plain twin" than usual.

"Awfully."

"Haven't you got a new one too?"

"No."

"Why not?"

"Well, that's where the 'bought' part of the tell comes in. She got Mr. Bliss to advance her some money. She had to have it. They all wear satin and things in the models' room. With what was over she got this frock. It's an old one that had gone into stock."

Catherine looked worried.

"I wish I hadn't bought that tell. Daddy would be very angry if he knew she had borrowed. He does so hate debt. I'm glad you had the sense not to."

"Well, it's really not so much sense, as it's not so easy for me. I could go to Miss Jones, but she'd have to ask Mrs. Renton, and she'd most likely say 'No'. Petronella just asked Mr. Bliss, and that was that."

"Does she see him more than you do?"

"Um. He designs dresses on her. You know, he makes a drawing first, and then sometimes when he's pleased with it he just has it made. Other times he pins a shape on her in cotton or something and designs like that. And sometimes it's with real stuff."

"On her?" Catherine looked puzzled. "What's she got on?"

Pauline giggled.

"It's quite neat, what they wear, but I wouldn't ask to see

82

it if I were you, or one day you'll tell Daddy and he'd have a fit."

Petronella came out of the house. The frock was blue. The colour of harebells. Made of some silk and wool material. It had perfect cut.

"Oh, dear," said Catherine, "she really is lovely."

Petronella looked inquiringly at Pauline.

"Did you get Mum to buy that tell?"

"She did," said Catherine severely, "and she shouldn't have. Daddy hates people borrowing."

Petronella didn't even bother to listen to this. She had the frock, and the tell was bought, and that was all that mattered.

"I think I look rather like Virginia Bruce in this. Do you like the way I've done my hair?"

Catherine laughed.

"You change it so often I never know what it was like before you changed it."

"I've been the whole afternoon doing this," said Petronella in a hurt voice. "Don't you ever look at films? If you did you'd see it's exactly like her."

"Are we being honoured with the new dress because the designer's coming to tea?"

"In a way. The girls, at least Betty and Eloise, thought it was a quarter of an inch too long. I thought I'd ask him. It's a good chance."

Pauline dug a hole in the lawn with a bit of stick.

"I think that's awfully mean. He must want a holiday on Sundays. Not just go on staring at more beastly clothes."

"He likes looking at me." Petronella was not bragging, merely stating a fact. "He often says so."

Pauline, hating herself, simply couldn't leave it at that.

"I'd much rather people wanted to talk to me than just stare."

"You wouldn't if you were me," Petronella said mildly. "Most people don't talk to me about interesting things. Sometimes when he talks about plays he's seen I wish he'd just look."

"Be quiet, darlings." Catherine got up. "I hear their car."

Ever since Lady Bliss had heard that David was coming for the week-end she had smelt a rat. Hers was a nose acutely adjusted to rat smelling. But even if it hadn't been adjusted at all she could hardly have missed this one. The cricket match at a nearby town! David said he knew the man who was getting up a scratch team. Well, he might do, but if it came to that he knew half the men in England who got up scratch teams. And it certainly was queer that this was the first summer since he was a child that he had played cricket in the neighbourhood. The only question in Lady Bliss's mind was, "Which twin was it?"

She got her answer the moment she stepped on to the Vicarage lawn. David did manage to shake hands with Catherine, he did manage a smile and "Hullo, Twin," to Pauline; then he felt his duty done. Never was any man more palpably bewitched.

Lady Bliss's reaction was exactly what Catherine's would have been if she had noticed anything, which she had not. She felt an urge to spoil Pauline. Throughout tea she chattered to her. She could not bear there to be a moment when she was not being talked to in case she should feel left out. Though how, thought Lady Bliss, could one twin fail to feel left out when the other twin was being so openly adored?

Catherine talked to David. He didn't mind, for Petronella sat between them, and talking across her it was absolutely necessary to look at her. Looking at her almost deprived him of speech. In her blue frock with the sun glinting on those pale curls, she was a sight to make any man giddy.

Pauline replied politely when there was any break for a reply in what Lady Bliss said. She looked now and again across at David. She saw his efforts to talk to Catherine. She saw just what an effect Petronella was having on him.

"Melted. That's how he looks," she thought sadly. "Melted. Just like butter by a fire."

Catherine pouring out tea, with one ear for Mark's step on the gravel, murmured happily to David. She found to her surprise he was interested in Women's Institutes. At least apparently he was, for he kept asking questions. She seemed to be talking a great deal, she thought, but if he liked it that was all right.

Petronella made an immense tea. She let her mind drift. Each time she bothered to listen to what they were all saying they were duller than before. Her mother on that awful Institute, nobody could want to talk about that. And Lady Bliss telling Pauline that she did not see enough of her, and saying she had some friends in London that she would like her to meet. She did hope, if Pauline had to meet the friends in London, she wouldn't have to go too. She knew just what they'd be like. They'd talk about gardens.

Mark came in when they'd nearly finished. Catherine turned to Petronella.

"Move to the chair the other side of Mr. Bliss, darling,

and let Daddy sit there." She smiled at David. "He likes a table to put his cup on. The grass isn't at all the same thing to him."

Mark was glad to see David. A case had recently come to his notice of a girl from his parish who had gone to work in London. The hours he had thought hard, and the rules arbitrary. Could David tell him exactly what arrangements he made about his own staff?

David tried. Not for worlds would he appear to Petronella's father the sort of cad who never bothered about the people he employed. Besides, it wasn't true. When he had first started in business he had learnt what standards of pay there were, and then improved on them. Every year an employee stayed their wages rose slightly. They had full pay while on holiday. But what on earth the minimum wage he paid was, and how each employee lived he hadn't the least idea. Or if he had he was quite incapable of thinking of it now while every inch of him ached to turn round and look at Petronella.

After tea Catherine took Lady Bliss off to look at the garden. Mark lit his pipe and David a cigarette.

"Would you like to go on being grand sitting in a chair, or lie on the ground?" Pauline asked. "If it's the ground you must come on the rug or you'll get all over grass whiskers. They're bad just now."

He looked across at her. She was lying on her tummy. Her face was towards him, her chin resting on her hands.

"Still worrying about my clothes?"

She nodded.

"You have lovely clothes. All the girls at the shop think so."

Petronella nodded.

"In the models' room we think your clothes are as nice as Herbert Marshall's."

"Who," inquired Mark, "is Herbert Marshall?"

Petronella turned to David.

"I can't make him learn. He hardly ever goes to see a picture and then only things like 'The Good Earth' and that dull one about the man who stopped people going mad when dogs bit them. I can't think why they ever make those sort."

David laughed.

"They don't often."

Petronella walked across the lawn.

"I bought this dress out of stock. Do you think it's too long?"

Mark got up.

"Perhaps I had better go before all you dress-makers get busy." He turned to David. "I like a quiet time before the service to go through my sermon."

Petronella pointed at David.

"When he came to church he used to draw in his Bible when you preached."

David looked embarrassed. What a very awkward thing for her to say to her father. Of course, she didn't know, or at least she didn't seem to, why he was so anxious to make a good impression. All the same, need she have dragged that up?

Mark shook David's hand.

"I dare say. The best of us, and I've never been that, are apt to be boring, I'm afraid. But what I remember about you is how you made runs for the village at cricket, and an exceedingly good coconut shy you ran one summer at the church fête. Good-bye."

David shook Mark's hand heartily.

"He's not a bad sort," he thought. "Funny I never noticed him then. Fancy his remembering about that coco-nut shy. Lucky!"

David got down on the rug by Pauline. Petronella had pulled the leg rest out from under her chair. She looked even more lovely, he thought, stretched out at full length. Like that play of Shakespeare's where the fairy queen went to sleep on a mossy bank. The words came back to him: "Never harm nor spell nor charm, come our lovely lady nigh." At least he thought it was that. "Lovely lady!" It might have been written for Petronella, only it ought to be "lovely child".

"If there are any raspberries," said Petronella, "bags I take them for the models' room."

"You had them last week," Pauline objected.

"Well, they're no good to you. There's only five of us. If you took them you'd have to give them to the whole shop."

David took his eyes off Petronella for a second.

"Why've you got to feed the multitude?"

Petronella wriggled more comfortably into her chair.

"She eats with them. All of them! All those drab girls in the workroom. I can't think how she can."

"They aren't drab." Pauline sat up on her haunches. "They're awfully nice. Mrs. Brown says they're as nice a lot in the workroom as you'd find anywhere."

Petronella made a face at David.

"You know what she'd mean by nice. Good. But however good you are it doesn't say you aren't drab."

David turned once more to Pauline.

"Why do you know the work-girls? You're in the showroom."

Petronella laid her skirt out on the chair where she could admire it.

"She isn't. She's runner for everybody. In the models' room we think it a shame."

Pauline sat up where she could catch Petronella's eye.

"It isn't. You know I like it."

Petronella smoothed her frock.

"It's no good looking angry. We do think it's a shame."

David swung round to face Pauline.

"What is it you do exactly?"

"She—" Petronella began.

David smiled at her over his shoulder.

"Give the other twin a chance." He patted Pauline's knee. "Come on, out with it."

Pauline leaned towards him.

"When you were little did you ever have bought tells?" He shook his head. "Well, it's when you ask somebody a question and the answer might mean a punishment. If you buy a tell you can't punish for it."

"What's that got to do with your job?"

"Only if you buy what it is you can't punish me."

"Well, that's safe. I shan't want to punish you anyway. I'll buy it."

David listened in shocked surprise to Pauline's description of her work. What on earth had Moira been thinking of? When he had agreed to take the twins he had quite clearly said they would have opportunities to get on. Whatever opportunities could Pauline have trotting up and down the stairs?

"My dear Twin, there's been some muddle. I don't know what came over Mrs. Renton, but she must have misunderstood what I wanted. Never mind, I'll put it right to-morrow."

Pauline stammered with indignation.

"You can't do that. You bought the tell."

"But you said that I couldn't punish you. Moving you to a better job won't be a punishment."

"To me it would. I like what I'm doing. You see, it's what I'm used to. I've done that sort of thing in a way always. You know, delivering confirmation veils, and finding out who can drive people to the old people's tea. At your shop it's exactly the same, only it's Mrs. Faucett-Eagles instead of the confirmation, and the Manton wedding instead of the old people's tea."

"She does like it," Petronella agreed. "She even likes the people. That awful Miss Blane, who says we make a mess of the dresses."

"Well, I expect you do," said Pauline, "and Miss Blane isn't awful. It's just she has indigestion. Anybody who felt as ill as she does would be cross sometimes."

"Well, I like her better than Miss Jones," Petronella agreed grudgingly. "She comes to our door at least a hundred times a day and says, 'Girls! girls! girls! What a noise! Mrs. Renton will be terribly vexed if she hears you.' And it's an awful lie, because we never do make a noise. At least, not often."

Pauline beat the ground with her hand in her indignation.

"How would you like to be her? Cursed by Mrs. Renton

90

for everything everyone else does, and you do make a terrible noise, I've heard you." Pauline flung round to David. "And she doesn't earn an awful lot, and out of it she has to keep a mother in an asylum."

"Well, I don't see how our being quieter would help her mother," Petronella argued. "It's just you're so soppy about everybody. Just giving them messages you don't see them as we do. You think that Miss Edwards is nice, but you should hear what the girls say. They say that when they are showing dresses she keeps them there hours longer than she need."

David looked up at Petronella.

"I must put in a word for poor Edwards. She's been with me since the beginning and she works like a Trojan."

"And all the time she's unhappy inside," Pauline added. "Because the man she was going to marry is out of work and can't get a job."

David stared at her. His voice was gentle.

"How do you know all these things? You know more about my people in three weeks than I've ever known."

"Well, Brownsy told me to start with, and then now I've got to know them they talk to me. There's somebody in the village going to make some tea in the autumn that might do Miss Blane's indigestion good. Then Miss Edwards hasn't exactly talked to me about Tom, but she said if she ever had the luck to marry the man she wanted to she wouldn't fuss with a big wedding, however rich she was, she'd just want to be married in what she had on." Pauline's voice dropped a little. "I think she's quite right."

"I don't." Petronella sat up. "When I marry I'm going to have a big silver bell hung over me like I saw in a film. And

I'm going to have the longest train anybody ever had and more bridesmaids."

Pauline pulled a daisy.

"Well, I hope you don't get your things at 'Reboux', these big weddings half kill everybody."

David laughed.

"You speak with feeling."

"Well, this Manton one has been awful."

"Never mind, it's all packed off now."

"Miss Jones says she won't sleep happy until the register's signed. She says she wakes up worrying something's forgotten."

Lady Bliss and Catherine came back.

"You really ought to see the garden, David," said Lady Bliss, who had been mellowed by a promise of a rare rock plant cutting. "After all," she thought, "if he's in that state about the girl he has only two alternatives, or at least, only two in a decent home like this. He's either got to marry her or get over her. The sooner he makes up his mind which the better, for really he's very dull in his present mood."

David got up. He held out a hand to Petronella.

"Come and show me the garden. I like my models to take exercise. It's good for their figures."

Petronella scowled.

"I do call that mean on a Sunday. I was awfully comfortable where I was. Why can't Pauline show you?"

"No, thank you," said Pauline firmly. She was adding a sprig of grass to the daisy and didn't look up.

"Come, too," David suggested, suddenly conscious that his grabbing of Petronella had been a bit obvious.

"No, thank you," she said again. This time her voice was

almost cross.

Catherine held out her hand to David.

"I may not see you when you come back. I have to go to church. I hope the girls are worth what you pay them—it seems an awful lot."

"They're certainly worth it. Pauline's been telling me more about my own work-people than I've ever known. I have an idea that she may have invented a job for herself."

"What?" Pauline rolled over and propped herself up on her elbows.

He leant down and took her face by the chin. He gave it an affectionate shake.

"You'll see."

"Do you really like looking at gardens?" said Petronella. "I simply hate it."

David slipped his arm through hers.

"I don't mind. Has it struck you at all that I like being with you?"

Petronella considered.

"No. I know you like looking at me. You've said so."

"More than just looking at you. Talking to you. Perhaps loving you."

"Goodness!" Petronella opened her enormous eyes. "No. Do you? I never loved anybody except Gary Cooper, and I've never met him, so that's different."

David made her stand still.

"Could you think about me for a moment? Could you ever be fond of me, do you think?"

"I don't know." Petronella looked worried. "Do you mean fond of you so as to go to bed with you?"

David laughed.

"What have you been reading?"

"Nothing. I never read. It's what Violet said. She said that was all any man wanted from any girl."

David made a face.

"Violet's a nasty bit of work. I wouldn't listen to her too much if I were you. I can't think why Moira keeps her. She says she's a good model."

"I like her," said Petronella, moving on. She stood beside a clump of delphiniums. In that dress against those flowers she was a dream.

David put his arm round her.

"Come on, duckie. If you stand against those flowers I shall kiss you."

Petronella looked up at him

"You can if you like."

"Would you like me to?"

"Well, I've never been kissed by a man except relations. I would like to be kissed like people are on the pictures."

"Petronella," David took her by the arms and turned her to face him, "have you been taking in a word I've been saying?"

"Yes." She nodded. "You said perhaps you loved me, and could I be fond of you."

"Well, could you?"

She looked vague.

"I don't know."

He dropped her arms. He leant forward and gave her a kiss on the tip of her nose.

"Perhaps you haven't seen enough of me. Will you come to dinners and theatres and things with me?"

Her eyes shone.

"Oh, yes. I'd love that."

"And presently I'll ask you again if you could care for me at all."

"All right." She turned.   "Have you seen enough of the garden? I do hate it, don't you?"

When David had gone the twins (Petronella out of the new dress) lay on the rug and ate some cherries they had found in the kitchen.

"How do you suppose it feels to love anybody?" said Petronella. "On the pictures it's the way people look. Do I look any different?"

"No. Why?" Pauline tried not to bark out the words.

"Only David asked me if I was fond of him, and I wondered if I was."

Pauline did not answer for a moment. Her voice was steady when she said:

"You'll know you are when you are."

"Will I?" Petronella took another cherry. "That's a good thing. Let's race at cherry bob."

CHAPTER 6

MOIRA SENT for Petronella. She was putting on her outdoor things to go and be photographed when the message arrived. Only Eloise was in the room. The others were in the showroom. Petronella took the message calmly, but Eloise was immensely interested.

"*She* never sees us just for nothing. Either she wants us to do something special, or else it's something we've done. I expect you moved and spoilt those last photographs."

Petronella combed her hair.

"I shouldn't wonder. First I went to the hairdresser and he took hours. Then I went to the photographers'. Miss Maud was there with six dresses. And they took about twenty photographs of each dress. It's a wonder I didn't faint right away. I felt awful."

"You ate a big enough lunch when you got back."

Petronella giggled.

"Well, I was tired, anyway. And if she's cross I shall ask her how she'd like a morning like that."

But Moira was anything but cross. All the Belton charm was to the fore, and there was masses of it when she wanted it.

"Good morning, Peter. I've got a party dining and dancing at the Savoy on Wednesday. I've a couple of extra men. I've asked Violet to come. Are you free?"

The Savoy was to Petronella just a name she knew from the wireless programmes. After listening in to dance music she wished she were there. She beamed at Moira.

"Oh, I'd love to come!"

"Give Violet your address. The car will call for you at a quarter to eight."

Petronella went back to the models' room. Betty and Violet were still showing. She sat down on the foot of Eloise's chair.

"Guess what *she* wanted."

"It wasn't the photographs?"

"No."

"Had you mucked up one of the dresses?"

"No." Petronella couldn't keep it back any longer. "She's asked me to go to dinner and to dance at the Savoy. She's asked Violet, too."

Eloise said nothing for a minute. Then she looked up.

"Well, I hope you enjoy yourself. Without sour grapes or anything, I don't mind telling you that Mrs. R. and Violet aren't my idea of good company."

"Violet isn't? But you like her."

"Who said so?"

"Well, I thought—"

"Well, you thought wrong. She's a very good model, and lots of fun, but I wouldn't trust her farther than I could throw her."

"Goodness! Why?"

"Ever heard of a copper's nark?" Petronella shook her head. "Well, it's the person who looks as if they were just ordinary people, but who really sneaks round and tells the police all they can find out."

Petronella was puzzled.

"But what's she got to do with police?"

Eloise sighed.

97

"In words of one syllable then, be careful what you tell Violet. It all goes back to Mrs. R."

"But I haven't anything to say Mrs. Renton can't hear."

Eloise sighed.

"Trying to tell you things is like explaining things to something at the Zoo. Don't you ever think, Peter?"

Petronella collected her gloves and bag.

"Not often. Things just happen, don't they?"

That night, on the way home, Petronella told Pauline of her invitation. Pauline was worried. They were at the bus stop at the time, and the usual number of people were staring at Petronella, so she waited till they were safely inside, strap-hanging, before she answered.

"Why did she ask you?"

"I told you, she had two extra men."

"Oh, well, I suppose it's all right. Only I don't like her much."

Petronella swung round on her strap. Crushed in the middle of the bus it was the first time anyone had seen her face. Now three men with seats leapt to their feet. Petronella smiled divinely and chose one.

Pauline paid no attention. Sooner or later Petronella was offered a seat every night. Sometimes she was, too; but not often. She was glad when she was not, because the men who travelled home with them always looked tired. "And perhaps," she thought, "they haven't as nice jobs as we have."

The worst of Petronella's getting a seat when she didn't was that Petronella went on talking just as if they were still standing next to each other. She took it for granted that the whole bus liked hearing what she had to say. The unfortunate thing, from Pauline's point of view, was that they usually did. She went straight on talking now.

"I don't see that it matters if you like people or not if they take you to the Savoy."

A look of envy came over every man's face. They couldn't afford the Savoy or anything like it. But how lucky for those who could. Practically every female face showed a wish to save. This lovely little creature with the pretty voice ought not to be at the mercy of marauding men. She ought to be petted and fussed over.

"We'll talk about it when we get in," said Pauline hurriedly.

There was a pause while the bus, which had stopped for traffic lights, suddenly rumbled on again. Petronella looked up at Pauline.

"I don't know why I was asked instead of Eloise or Mary or Betty, whoever they might be."

Men and women alike, they smiled.

"I do wish I'd something nice to wear," Petronella went on. "Those white frocks Mum had made for us are all wrong. I knew they would be."

The bus looked sympathetic, though their sympathy was tinged with the thought that Petronella would look nice in anything.

Pauline could bear it no more. She was tired and they were only as far as Harrods, but it seemed mean to discuss the clothes her mother had bought in front of everybody. She caught at Petronella's hand.

"Come on, let's walk."

"Why on earth get out here?" said Petronella, when they were on the pavement. "It's miles yet."

"Because I couldn't bear your talking like that in front of everybody."

Petronella raised her eyebrows.

"But if they were interested I don't mind them hearing, and if they weren't they needn't listen. Now we'll have to hurry because I want Aunty-mum to iron my white dress."

Petronella stood in the middle of the bedroom and turned slowly round.

" 'Ou does look a pettums," said Miss Williams.

"It looks awfully nice," said Pauline.

"It looks ghastly," said Petronella. "It's got no line and no cut. But I expect I'll enjoy myself just the same."

Petronella did enjoy herself. The party were already sitting at a table at the top of the steps leading to the restaurant when Violet and Petronella arrived. They were drinking cocktails. There was another woman of Moira's age, two older men, and two young men.

"Why," asked the woman, whose name was Ruth, in a whisper to Moira, "the two youths? Have you taken to cradle-snatching, darling?"

"I've two girls coming, my sweet," Moira retorted. "And if there was a kick for me in cradle-snatching I'd snatch, as you know, damn well. As it happens there isn't."

"And where's David to-night?" Ruth inquired.

Moira took a sip of her cocktail.

"Out of town for two days. He's staying with the Pulfords in Scotland. Their squinting daughter is being married in August. He's gone to see what he can design in which she won't look too appalling."

"What are the names of the girls who are coming?" asked

one of the men.

"They are two of my models. You just call them Violet and Peter. Violet's dark and Peter's fair." She looked up. "Oh, there they are."

The whole table looked up. Violet was shepherding Petronella out of the ladies' cloakroom. Catherine, going by a *Vogue* and personal inclination, had chosen organdie for the twins. The dress was not smart. What in *Vogue* had possessed chic and finish, had the fine edge of its charm removed by the time it was copied by the little dressmaker Catherine employed to make her own and the girls' dresses. But even as it was, the frock had merit. It accentuated the fact that Petronella was very young. Its *bouffant* white skirts billowed round her childishly, held in at the waist by swathed velvet ribbons. There was nothing in the dress to take away from her loveliness, and certain qualities in its freshness and whiteness to enhance it.

"Good God!" said Ruth.

"Is what I see what I see?" asked one of the elder men.

"It's all right," said the other one, "it's true, and it's coming here."

The two younger men said nothing. One's hand shook so that he upset his cocktail, the other turned scarlet to the tips of his ears.

"This is Violet," said Moira, "and this is Peter."

The whole evening enchanted Petronella. Everybody, she thought, was so nice. The two men on either side of her saw that she had a second helping of almost everything at dinner, especially the iced pudding.

"I know I'm eating an awful lot," she apologized to the table generally. "But if you lived where I live and ate Miss

Williams' awful dinners every night you'd be hungry."

"Very sensible," said one of the older men. "Hate all this banting."

"Oh, I don't bant," said Petronella, laughing. "Why should I?"

"I shouldn't brag," Ruth suggested. "The gods might hear. I believe they can be jealous."

"Gods!" Petronella looked puzzled.

"Don't worry," Moira said, "she's only teasing. And as for the meals, I dare say this won't be the only one you eat in a restaurant."

"No, it won't," Petronella agreed. "Mr. Bliss said would I come out with him."

Ruth turned to her next door neighbour.

"Daylight at last," she whispered. "I wondered what all this motherly stuff for her models meant. I bet he's very épris."

"Don't blame him," the man murmured. "Should be myself, only I've outgrown flappers."

Moira, with generations of Belton breeding behind her, showed not a flicker of annoyance.

"And I don't suppose David will be the only one," she said lightly, giving the two young men a smile.

Ruth waited until the conversation became general, then she nudged Moira.

"I'd hate to be inquisitive, my pet, but what's the game?"

Moira raised her eyebrows.

"What do you mean?"

"Well, why hand this girl about on a plate as if she was the eldest of your six daughters and you had to get her off before the other five emerged from the schoolroom?"

102

Moira smiled into her champagne glass.

"If I have a motive I'm not telling you."

Ruth shrugged her shoulders.

"Well, you're wasting your time. Anybody who looks like that girl doesn't need hawking. She'll be killed in the rush. So if that's what you want, sit back and take it easy."

Moira lit a cigarette. She gave Ruth an enigmatic glance.

"You're a fanciful creature."

Ruth took a drink of champagne.

"Am I hell? I know you."

Moira sent Petronella home at half-past twelve. She had too much interest in the firm to let its best photographic model sit up till all hours. One of the two young men offered to drive her. Both the young men 'and one of the older ones made dates with her. Each of them made them secretly while they were dancing with her. Petronella, who saw nothing requiring secrecy in the arrangements, covered them all with confusion when she said good-bye to Moira.

"Thank you so much. I have enjoyed it. I suppose you haven't a piece of paper and pencil, have you? He's asked me to dance, and he's taking me to dinner and a theatre, and he's taking me somewhere. I think I ought to put the days down."

The three "he's" looked sheepish and fumbled in their pockets. Moira was before them.

"What about the menu card, darling? Here's a pencil." She looked up. "One of you men might send her an engagement-book. I'll put the dates down. Who's asked her for what? Don't all speak at once."

Ruth watched Petronella with her escort thread her way

through the tables. She made the utterly unselfconscious exit of real beauty. At every table heads turned. Every face lit up as she passed. Even in the blazing lights of the restaurant it was as if a more powerful light passed through the room, and with its going left dusk behind. She sighed.

"I don't know what Moira's game is," she said to the table generally, "but I suspect heaven watches over anything quite as lovely and quite as stupid as that. Special guardianship, you know, like they say drunkards get."

Pauline cried after Petronella had driven off. Without staring facts in the face she couldn't help seeing that she was getting nothing. It was not that she so desperately wanted to go to the Savoy; as a matter of fact she wouldn't have cared to go in a party of Moira's. But she too had a new frock, and somehow it seemed awfully dull to be sitting in your bedroom while your twin went out to a party.

There was a knock on the door. Pauline sat up, blew her nose, and scrubbed at her eyes.

"What is it?" she called out noisily.

It was the maid.

"Please, Miss, there's a gentleman on the phone asking for Miss Petronella. I said she'd gone out and he said could he speak to you. Mr. Bliss he said his name was."

"David!" Pauline jumped off the bed, threw open the door and tore down the stairs. The telephone was by the front door. She picked up the receiver. "Hullo, is that you?"

A laugh came over the phone.

"If by 'Is that you' you mean is it David Bliss, the answer is yes. Where's your sister?"

"She's out. She's gone to a party at the Savoy. Mrs. Renton asked her."

"Moira!" David, at the other end of the line, could have sworn. Blast Moira, what did she want, carting the girl around? Once she was seen about half the men in town would be wanting to know her. "Bother," he said, "I'm just back from Scotland. I wondered if she'd come and have a bite with me somewhere."

"Oh!" With all her effort to sound casual it was a very dreary little "oh" that came down the phone. "Well, I'll tell her. I'm sure she'll be awfully sorry she couldn't."

"Thanks," said David. He was about to hang up the receiver when a thought struck him. "I say, Paul, I want a talk with you. I suppose you couldn't come, could you?"

Pauline didn't know the meaning of false pride. She quite realized she was a poor substitute for Petronella, but what did she care? She'd have this evening at least for her own.

"Oh, may I? I've had dinner." She looked round the hall to make sure Miss Williams wasn't about. "But it wasn't nice, just cottage pie and tinned peaches and custard."

"Ugh! Could you forget about it and start all over again?"

"Easily."

"Right. I'll be round for you in about a quarter of an hour."

"I say, wait a minute." Excitement had made Pauline breathless. "Where are we going? I mean, what ought I to wear?"

"Anything. We'll just pop into a grill."

"It's no good talking all London to me like that. I don't know what a grill is."

David laughed.

"Well, wear day things. I'll be seeing you."

David's car nosed its way along Piccadilly. He smiled down at Pauline.

"What are you looking at?"

"All the lights. I've never been here in the evening. You know, until we came to work for you we'd hardly ever been away from Farlynge. We'd seen 'Peter Pan' and the circus at Brighton. And every year we go to Devonshire for a month, but then we stay in places smaller than Farlynge."

"Rather fun in a way." David turned his car down the Haymarket. "You've such lots of things you've never done."

"Almost everything," Pauline agreed contentedly. "Do you know, this is the first time I've ever been out alone with a man who wasn't a relation?"

David's face was serious.

"There are some funny customers about. You must be careful. Both of you."

Pauline didn't answer. It was quite obvious it was Petronella he was worrying about, and nothing could make her careful. It was just luck with her how things turned out.

They went into the Carlton Grill-room.

"What would be a good dinner, Charles," David asked the *maître d'hôtel*, "for Miss Lane? She's had one dinner she didn't like and now she's going to start all over again."

Charles smiled at Pauline. He handed her one menu while he considered another himself.

"I suppose," said Pauline, "I couldn't have lobster, could I?"

"Why not?" David looked up at Charles. "Cardinal, I think."

"And then," Pauline went on, "could I have an ice, a strawberry one?"

David nodded gravely.

"Lobster and strawberry ice. Very easy. Now for me—" He and Charles went into a technical discussion.

The wine waiter came up. David opened the wine card.

"Do you drink, Twin?"

Pauline leant her chin on her hands.

"Yes. I'd like lemonade, the fizzy sort."

He raised an eyebrow at her.

"I don't think it goes very well with lobster."

Pauline looked at him and the wine waiter.

"Isn't it lucky I've got the sort of inside everything goes in, even green apples?"

The wine waiter had children of his own. He smiled at her.

"Fizzy lemonade," he said gravely.

"I do wish this had happened next week instead of this week," Pauline observed when they were alone. "I'm buying that green frock with the green pleated coat, in stock. I'm afraid I'm not grand enough to come out with you in this."

David looked at her. She had on a simple navy blue frock and coat and a navy straw hat. His trained eye knew they were ready-made and had not cost much, but the effect of her in the things he thought charming. It was vaguely reminiscent of a school uniform. The school effect was enhanced by herself. As always she made him feel things were fun in the way they had been fun when he was a boy. Eating dinner with her was not taking a girl out to dine. It was as if she had the key to the gate back to childhood.

This meal was not dinner in the Carlton Grill, it was a stolen picnic with everything that was indigestible spread on a big handkerchief because they hadn't a table-cloth.

"Was it nice in Scotland?" Pauline asked.

"Awful. Never be a dress-designer. The Pulford girl squints."

"Is that why you're back early? Couldn't you bear it any more—you weren't coming till tomorrow, were you?"

He didn't wonder at her accurate knowledge of his movements. He had no conception that to her each day's work was a burden unless he were under the roof. He only thought of himself. Of the feeling of desperation that had seized him at the thought of yet another night without a sight of Petronella. His cocktail was brought at that minute. It spared him an immediate answer. He took a sip of his drink.

"London called," he said lightly.

"Goodness!" thought Pauline "He came back early specially to see Petronella. What a shame! I expect he's awfully bored having me instead."

"I expect Petronella will be able to come next time."

David looked up startled.

"Did she tell you what I said to her on Sunday?"

"Um."

David had not thought of discussing his feelings about Petronella with Pauline or anyone, but since she had started it was an enormous relief.

"Do you think she likes me at all?"

Pauline drank some of her lemonade while she thought of a kind answer.

"Not yet. But I expect she will. You see, since she was

little she's meant to marry a film star, and it takes time to get over the feeling."

"Does she talk about me much?"

Pauline was torn. She hated lying, and she hated hurting.

"Of course. You see, it's the shop we mostly talk about, and you're the most important person there."

"Yes, but about me apart from the shop?"

Pauline stared at her napkin.

"She isn't a person who talks about people. That's where we're different. I like knowing every single thing about people. Like that Sunday when you told me about you when you were a little boy."

"You don't think it means that she doesn't care because she doesn't show it?"

Pauline leant across to him.

"No. You know, I simply can't imagine Petronella showing she cared about anybody."

David lit a cigarette.

"You mean she's reserved. She doesn't show what she feels?"

Pauline was surprised that anybody could know Petronella five minutes and think a thing like that. Ever since she was a baby she had shown exactly what she felt, quite regardless of where she was or who was there. Boredom, and wanting things, and being pleased with things. But if David liked to think she was reserved she thought perhaps it would be a good thing. If somebody you are fond of takes no interest in you perhaps it's a comfort to say they're reserved.

"Something like that," she agreed vaguely. She fidgeted with a knife "As we are talking about her there's something

I wanted to say to you. She said you were going to take us both to the theatre one night. Well, there isn't any need. I know you're being polite. That you'd rather not have me."

He looked at her embarrassed face. Oddly that little speech recalled a scene when he was a small boy of fourteen. He had been asked to play in the Farlynge cricket team in his summer holidays. He had been overjoyed at first. Then doubts had crept in. Somebody was standing down for him. Either Bates at the garage, or Mr. Blow, his aunt's agent. Bates was a knock-out left-handed bowler when he bowled straight. Mr. Blow was about the best fielder they had. He went to the captain, who was the local baker, and, looking just as Pauline looked now, tried to explain that he was glad he'd been asked, but he knew they'd be glad if he didn't accept. The captain had been grand, he had heard him in silence and then said, "Maybe you're right, Master David. But most matches somebody falls out. Maybe you'll be twelfth man." He smiled at her now, as the captain had smiled.

"I like being with you too. But of course you're right, two's company under the circumstances. But perhaps some nights you'll come out with me on your own. Will you?"

She beamed.

"Of course I'd love it. I'm so glad you said that. I was afraid you were going to give one of those grown-up polite lies, and say of course you wanted me just as much as her."

David remembered the glow with which he had left his cricket captain. He too had been afraid of grown-up prevarication.

"I shouldn't think many people lie to you," he said, and added, "Look, here's your lobster."

"That," Pauline remarked after her second helping of strawberry ice, "is one of the nicest meals I ever ate."

"Good." He ordered coffee and lit a cigarette. "Now the big business of eating is over, I want to talk to you. Do you really want to go on running about my shop?"

She nodded.

"Yes. I'm very useful."

"So I should imagine. But by next month the rush is over. I think by then you ought to move into the showroom. You'd make a good saleswoman."

"Well, of course, if there isn't a rush they won't want a runner. It's a pity. I do like knowing everybody."

"That's just what I want to talk to you about. Going up to Scotland on Monday I was thinking about our talk on Sunday afternoon. I ought to know more about my staff, and do more for them. What do they think of me?"

"They don't think of you at all except in the models' room," Pauline said candidly. "You see, it's Mrs. Renton who matters to them."

David smoked a moment in silence.

"I've had a conscience stirring. Ought one to employ a whole lot of people and leave it to somebody else to see they get along all right?"

"I don't think so." Pauline shook her head. "If it was me, whoever I had working for me I'd know all about them. Just think, somebody might be ill and not have the money for an operation and you'd never know."

"They could go to Miss Jones," he said weakly.

Pauline looked scornful.

"They could go to her, and she'd go to Mrs. Renton. Would you like to have to ask Mrs. Renton to help you about anything?"

David raised his eyebrows.

"You don't like her?"

Pauline made a pellet of her bread.

"Daddy says everybody has got nice things about them if you look. The trouble is I've only seen her twice, and then the nice things weren't showing, and I hadn't time to look."

"Don't the workers like her?"

Pauline looked amazed at such ignorance.

"Goodness, no."

David waited a moment while their coffee was served. Then he said:

"I imagine a good manageress, and Moira is that, is never very popular. But what you say adds to an idea I had. How would it be if you made a list of any special things which crop up and tell me privately? I might be able to help."

"What sort of things?"

"Like you told me on Sunday. Edwards' man being out of a job, I—"

"Oh!" Pauline seized his hand across the table. "Will you find him one? Then she can be married."

David laughed. He gave her hand a brotherly squeeze. "I haven't seen the fellow yet. Don't know what he can do. Maybe he's a waster."

"He's not. His name's Tom and he's a French polisher, only people don't use those much now."

"I see. Then there's Jones. I might be able to shift her mother. I must find out if she's happy where she is. Then perhaps old Blane had better see a specialist—"

"Gosh," said Pauline admiringly. "You are going to do a lot. And I'm sure I can find plenty more."

He took a sip of coffee.

"Go ahead and find them. I don't say I'll help, but I might."

It was nearly eleven when they got back to the Cromwell Road. David looked at his watch in surprise.

"We've been nearly three hours over dinner. It feels like half an hour."

"That," said Pauline earnestly, "is because you've been so interesting."

He looked down at her smiling. He felt extraordinarily soothed by his evening. He didn't feel as though he'd had an evening in town after a long, tiring journey. He felt as though he'd been for a country walk. That they had dined at some village pub. He took hold of her by both arms and gave her a squeeze.

"You're an extraordinarily nice person, Pauline. Come out with me again soon."

Her back was to the street lamp. He couldn't see the pathetic twist of her mouth. He only heard what seemed a cheerful ring in her voice.

"Any time you can't get Petronella I'll come. How's that?"

He squeezed her again.

"Understanding, aren't you? Good night."

CHAPTER 7

AFTER THAT first party at the Savoy it was a case of taking
your place in the queue to go out with Petronella. At once
she became a figure in the night-clubs and restaurants.
Very few people knew her name, but everybody knew her
by sight, and quite a few knew who she was.

"Look, my dear, there's that lovely girl. She's a model at
'Reboux'. Isn't she too beautiful!"

All the *restaurateurs*, night-club owners, and *maîtres
d'hôtels* knew her. She was one of those people that the
whole of their training had taught them to spot. Useful
now because she brought men to eat and drink at their
tables. Certainly worth making a fuss of because you never
knew what might happen to a girl with a face like that. She
might marry a duke, or a millionaire. At every gala night in
any dancing place the best of the gifts and novelties went to
her.

"Our bedroom," said Pauline in disgust, "looks more like
a nursery every day. I can't think what you want the things
for."

Petronella looked round at the collection of dolls, paper
hats and toys.

"I don't really, but people give them to me. I can't throw
them away, can I?"

David, by dint of booking her well ahead, managed to get
a couple of nights a week with her. He usually took her to a
cinema. The first time they went out this was followed by
the Savoy Grill for supper. She seemed to enjoy it, for as
usual half the stage, film and literary lights of London were

there. He liked it because it gave him a chance to talk to her. To try to get to know her. But somehow the Savoy Grill was a failure. For all his struggling conversation ran dry. He simply could not take an interest in the home life of the film stars, or what Betty, Violet, Eloise and Mary thought about film stars; and Petronella had nothing else to talk about. As for Petronella, she summed up what she thought of the evening on her way home. David said:

"Don't forget Wednesday is mine. We'll do another film."

"All right," she agreed, "but don't let's have supper there. Let's go where there's a band."

Pauline began to go out a little too. Once or twice Petronella's parties wanted an extra girl. She made two men friends out of these occasions. They were both a lot older than she was, and liked good food and somebody to talk to while they ate it. Pauline was perfect for the job. She listened entranced to what had happened on the Stock Exchange from one of them, and to grumbles about his wife from the other. Where she failed from their point of view was on the way home. Nothing would make her allow them to kiss her in the taxi.

"But why not?" the Stock Exchange asked. "A kiss won't hurt you."

Pauline considered the point.

"I think kissing people's only nice when you're fond of them."

"Aren't you at all fond of me?"

Pauline didn't want to hurt his feelings, but really, she thought, men were awfully queer.

"I'm afraid not."

Both men went on asking her out in spite of her failure as a kisser, for there was never a more sympathetic listener. Both hoped, with masculine pertinacity, that after a time she'd weaken. After all, they thought, they could give the little thing a good time if only she'd be sensible. And after all, what did she want but a good time?

"Do all those men and boys you go out with try and kiss you on the way home?" Pauline asked Petronella.

Petronella opened surprised eyes.

"Of course. At least, David doesn't."

Pauline's heart leapt at that information.

"Do you let them?"

"Of course."

"But why? Don't you hate it?"

Petronella considered this question.

"I don't think about it at all. They just do it. I just sit."

When Moira's friend Ruth said that she suspected heaven watched over anything quite as lovely and stupid as Petronella, she stumbled on a truth. Petronella herself was so obliging that she would have done anything anyone asked her. But this very quality in her made her various friends take care of her. Besides which, the one thing they all wanted was marriage. There might be girls with whom a more temporary arrangement was possible, but not Petronella. Each man burst with a mixture of pride and jealousy every time he took her out. Pride in that he was with her, the envied of all, and jealousy because of the piercing male eyes fixed upon her. Who could say that one of them might not snatch the prize? Each of them saw in his dreams a nice crisp marriage licence. And when they had got it there would be no more dancing for Petronella.

No more sharing her loveliness with every man who could afford to eat and drink at expensive places. Four walls for her, and a well-shut door; and the satisfaction of saying, "This perfect thing is mine."

The trouble in all these schemes was Petronella. As far as could be seen she had no preferences. She let each one order her large unwholesome meals of her own choosing. She let each one tremble as he put his arms round her to dance with her. She turned her enormous eyes on each one of them in the intervals of dancing and talking about Hollywood. And she suffered each to kiss her unceasingly all the way home.

Moira, behaving uncommonly like a spider sitting on its web, watched Petronella and waited. July passed, and August. Usually London was empty of men in August, but this year a surprising number were what they called "just passing through". Certainly Petronella went out as much as usual. David, cursing himself for a fool, put off his holiday. He said he had to get on with the autumn designs. Pauline, who had stopped running and was in the showroom, filling the places of the various girls on holiday, knew how little designing he did. Often his door was open, and then she would see him walking restlessly up and down, smoking cigarette after cigarette. He looked ill too, it was obvious he wasn't sleeping.

Once in the early weeks of August David asked Pauline to dine. It was a hot night. He took her to Ranelagh and they sat outside and talked. Pauline would have been glad to talk about Petronella if it would help him, but he stopped her.

"I suspect I'm all kinds of a fool, Twin. I'll just have to

get out of it in my own way."

That was the night she wore her green frock with the green pleated coat.

"I say," said David when he saw her, "don't you look a treat of raspberries."

She looked down at herself proudly.

"It's the first time I've had it on. Now I'm saving for an evening frock. The only one I've got is white, and it's looking pretty awful."

He smiled, the placid smile he had nowadays for nobody but her.

"Tell me when you've got it, and we'll give it an evening out."

It was the day after Pauline's dinner with David that Moira sent for Violet. Eloise, Betty and Mary were having their holidays, so she and Petronella were alone in the models' room. Violet yawned and got out of her chair.

"Wonder what *she* wants. There can't be a customer. There never is in August. I can't think why she doesn't go away. Usually it's fun. She goes, and Mr. Bliss, and we do what we like."

Moira was at her desk. She looked up and smiled.

"Come in, Violet, and sit down. Cigarette?"

Violet took the cigarette. As she lit it she thought, "There's nothing wrong, anyway."

"I've sent for you," said Moira, "for a little private talk. What do you think of Petronella?"

Violet was always conscious which side the butter was on her bread. That Moira's nose was out of joint was whispered amongst those in the know.

118

"Well," she said cautiously, "I've been trying to teach her to model as you told me. She slouches rather."

"Not as a model. As a person. I've had rather bad reports of her."

"Liar," thought Violet.

"I understand that she's not a very good influence in your room."

"Isn't she?" Violet was too surprised to be tactful.

"No," Moira went on calmly. "I should, between you and me, be glad of an excuse to dismiss her."

"I bet you would," thought Violet.

"There are, as you know, very few things we dismiss for. Except wearing the firm's clothes outside. I suppose you've never known her do that?"

"No."

"But she might," Moira suggested.

"Yes."

"If she does will you let me know?"

Violet got up. It was clear what was expected of her.

"Yes, Mrs. Renton."

"Thank you." Moira tapped the ash off her cigarette. "Oh, by the way, I've told Miss Jones to give you a little rise. You'll find it in your envelope on Friday."

Moira, plagued all her life by dress bills, had not gauged Petronella wrongly. She had unobtrusively kept an eye on what the girl bought out of stock. She knew that was all she could be buying, for her salary was mortgaged up to the hilt. It was a rule at "Reboux" that the showroom and model girls could owe the firm on clothes which had been much worn by the models and gone into stock. Their debts,

119

however, were not allowed to exceed ten pounds. Petronella was still making weekly payments on the five pounds she had borrowed when she bought a green evening dress. That was followed almost at once by a blue one.

"How much does Peter owe the firm?" Moira asked Miss Jones.

Miss Jones consulted a ledger.

"Eight pounds."

Moira's voice was maternal.

"I don't think there's anything in the stockroom at two pounds, but tell them on the quiet I don't want her to buy any more. It is such a mistake, I think, for these young girls to get into debt. It can get them into all kinds of messes."

"All right, Mrs. Renton," Miss Jones agreed. But her eyes were on stalks as she said it. Mrs. Renton turning moralist! Mrs. Renton guarding young girls! There was something very queer about it.

Thanks to the slavish care Miss Williams spent on them, Petronella's three evening dresses stood up far better than could have been expected to the life they led. The white organdie was the first to go. That left just the blue and the green. They struggled manfully against being danced in, and crushed in cars and taxis on alternate nights. But there came a day when one of them had to go to the cleaners.

"Now we must be careful of 'ittle frockums this evening," said Miss Williams, feeling more than usual as if she were seeing to the toilet of her Pekinese. "Aunty-mum has had to send pwetty frock to be made all nice-ums again."

But to Petronella there was no such word as "careful". Things happened or they didn't. In this case what

120

happened was a tear. Getting out of the car, the material caught on something and was ripped.

At breakfast the next morning Petronella brought the dress to Miss Williams

"Could you mend this? I have to wear it to-night."

Miss Williams looked at the tear just as she looked at shoes chewed past redemption by the Pekinese.

"Naughty, naughty! Aunty-mum isn't a conjurer. This poor, poor frockums is spoilt. It will have to go to Mr. Invisible Mender."

"Gosh!" said Petronella. "What'll I wear tonight? What's the white like?"

Miss Williams made a clicking sound.

"Such a dirty, dirty little girl. Poor white frockums is all spoilt."

Petronella turned to Pauline.

"Can I borrow yours?"

"No, thank goodness," said Pauline "I expect I'd have lent it to you if I wasn't going out, but I am."

"Gosh!" Petronella observed gloomily to her porridge.

Betty was back from her holiday. Petronella went to her.

"I suppose you couldn't lend me a frock to wear to-night? Mine are being cleaned or mended." Betty laughed.

"After a fortnight at Folkestone, old dear, a girl hasn't a frock. Just a nice suit-case of bits waiting to be sewn together."

Petronella looked sadly at Violet.

"And you're too tall, even if you'd lend one. Gosh, I am in a mess."

Violet waited till Betty was out of the room, then she came and sat on Petronella's chair.

"I'll tell you something if you promise not to tell anybody. There's no need to fuss if you're a frock short. Just borrow it from stock."

"But I can get sent away for taking one."

"You can. But they never find out. It's easy as winking Just sneak one in a parcel and put it back the next morning. I'd take the black net if I were you. It won't mark."

Petronella's face lit up.

"I'd love to. I'll look like Joan Crawford in it."

"Well, go on, take it."

"All right," agreed Petronella, "I will."

After lunch Violet went down and knocked on Moira's door.

"Well? " said Moira.

"It's about Petronella." Violet flushed. She was glad of her rise, but she felt a cad. "She's borrowing the black net to-night."

Moira's face showed nothing.

"Thank you," she said quietly. "You did perfectly right to tell me."

Consequences never bothered Petronella. But it did strike her that if Pauline saw the black net frock she would be sure to argue, which would be tiresome. Lots of people did borrow clothes, as Violet had pointed out, and nobody minded because nobody knew. But Pauline wasn't the person to see a thing like that; she would be sure to make a fuss. She wouldn't see an obvious thing like a person not being able to go about naked. The best way was not to let her know anything about it. She would put the frock on in the bathroom.

But Petronella was no strategist. Pauline, she knew, was being fetched by her Stock Exchange man at eight. She herself was being fetched by someone in the Coldstreams at a quarter to eight. She was late dressing, as usual, so it was twenty minutes to eight when, with her bag in her hand, her evening coat over her arm, and the net frock in a rustling paper parcel, she sneaked to the bedroom door, expecting Pauline not to notice.

Pauline, of course, could hardly fail to see that her sister was going out to dine and dance dressed, as far as she could see, in the shortest of shell-pink panties and a fragmentary wisp of net as a brassière.

"Goodness!" she said, staring. "Are you being Dorothy Lamour to-night?"

Petronella fidgeted.

"You are stupid. Of course I'm going to put on a frock."

"Well, which? The green's at—"

Pauline stopped. "What's in that parcel you brought back from the shop?"

Petronella stood on one leg.

"What's it got to do with you?"

Pauline left the dressing-table where she was doing her hair. She came across to Petronella.

"You haven't taken one from the shop?"

Petronella disliked her tone.

"You needn't sound as if it was so awful. Lots of girls do."

Pauline was appalled.

"But it's stealing."

"Not to me it isn't." Petronella looked unctuous. "What's wrong to one person is right to another. I heard Daddy say that."

"Not about stealing, he didn't. That was about playing cards on Sundays."

"But I don't call it stealing. I call it borrowing."

There was a knock on the door. The maid had come to say there was a gentleman downstairs waiting for Miss Petronella.

"There!" said Petronella, dragging the string off the parcel. "You've made me late."

"Gosh!" Pauline was looking at the frock. "It's the black net. I do wish you hadn't taken that one. I was going to buy it as soon as I'd saved enough."

"Well, you still can." Petronella dragged the frock over her head. "I'm only borrowing it. Do me up."

Pauline turned Petronella with her back facing the light.

"Well, I will, because you'll only get Aunty-mum if I don't. But I still think it's stealing. And I expect you'll get caught, and then we'll both have to leave the shop."

"Well, who cares! We could go somewhere else."

Pauline paused with her hand on a hook.

"Wouldn't you care?"

Petronella wriggled.

"Do hurry up. No, of course I wouldn't care. 'Reboux's' isn't the only dress-shop in London."

Pauline fastened the last of Petronella's hooks. She watched her dash out of the room, slamming the door. She went back to the glass to finish her hair.

"She isn't getting a bit fond of him," she told herself, "or of course she'd mind leaving. I wonder if she even knows how fond he is of her?" She turned to her bed and picked up her organdie frock. She made a face at it. After the black net it looked painfully provincial. "It does seem mean," she said out loud, "that I had to be both the plainest and the one with the conscience. Plain faces ought to have no consciences. That would balance things a bit."

Pauline was woken at seven o'clock the next morning by most depressing sounds. She opened an unwilling eye. She got out of bed and went to Petronella's assistance at the basin. When all was over and she had an emerald green Petronella safely back in bed, she sat down beside her.

"Is it something you ate?"

Petronella lay flat on her back. She shut her eyes.

"Don't shake the bed or I'll do it again. Ate and drank, I think I ate an awfully big dinner, and then we danced. Then John, that's the man I was with, said I'd better drown my sorrows."

"What sorrows?"

"It wasn't my fault," Petronella explained weakly. "The waiter upset some ice-pudding on it. I washed out the place but it still shows rather."

"Do you mean on the black net dress?"

"Um. Oh, goodness, don't talk about it. I feel simply awful anyway."

"You look it," Pauline agreed. "I expect castor oil would—"

Suspicious sounds from Petronella stopped her.

"Oh, well, don't think about it till you're better. But you know, you must get well in time to go to the shop. Keeping the frock to-day as well as wearing it last night really would be stealing."

"Shut up," said Petronella. "I'm going to be sick again."

But when it was time to go to work there could be no

question of Petronella getting up. She was still flat on her back, very green looking, and as Miss Williams kept murmuring, "So sickums, us can't keep nothing down."

"It's no good," Petronella whispered. "You'll have to take back the frock."

Nobody could be outspoken with anything so feeble and pale as Petronella, but Pauline was so dismayed she had to make some protest.

"Oh, it is mean. Fancy making me."

The ghost of a smile flicked across Petronella's face.

"I shall laugh if Mrs. Renton catches you."

Pauline worked off some of her rage on the brown paper in which she was packing the frock. She folded down the edges as if she were crushing a snake.

"All right, it may seem funny to you, but how would you like it if I borrowed a frock and made a mess on it, and then drank too much champagne and ate too much iced pudding and was sick and made you take it back?"

Another spasm was passing through Petronella's inside.

"Fetch Aunty-mum," she gasped, "and tell her she'd better be quick."

Moira had stayed on late the night before. She had sent for Miss Blane and Miss Edwards. Miss Jones had to remain in the building as long as she did as a matter of routine. Miss Blane had just been putting on her coat when the summons came. Her summer holiday (a fortnight at Bexhill) had done her indigestion good. She was struggling to hold on to the little improvement. To get home as quickly as possible and relax. The call from Moira she thought most unkind.

"Inconsiderate creature," she muttered as she went down the stairs. "She knows Miss Maud's away and I've my hands full."

Miss Edwards was meeting Tom. Nobody wants to be late when they are meeting the man they're fond of, particularly when he's out of work and needs his spirits kept up. Her holiday was starting next week. She had managed to persuade him she did not need to get right away this year. That it would be more fun for her to take her holiday in London, and then they could go off hiking every day.

"Oh, dear," she thought, "I hope *she* doesn't keep us late. With Tom borrowing the road map and all. He'll be sure to have spent the day writing down the roads and be wanting to show it to me."

Miss Jones heard Moira's bell with a resigned sigh. She could not take her holiday till Moira took hers. Really, between being so tired and finding the journeys to the asylum more of a strain than usual and Moira so difficult, she often wished she had the courage to make an end of things. Life seemed particularly unattractive.

Moira saw at once that the three women were resentful. On this occasion she cared, as she wanted them on her side.

"I do hate to keep you," she said sweetly, "but I want your help. A friend wants to buy a frock out of stock. I thought you two (here she smiled at Miss Blane and Miss Edwards) "knew what was there and might help. It's for her daughter. A girl of eighteen."

Miss Edwards looked at Miss Blane. Both their faces had the fixed appearance of people whose inward eyes are raking through cupboards.

"Is the little yellow still about?" said Miss Blane.

Miss Edwards shook her head.

"All messed up. It wouldn't do for a friend of Mrs. Renton's." She turned to Moira. " Would she wear white?"

Moira laughed.

"No. Like all girls she's afraid of looking childish. She'd much rather wear black."

Miss Blanc unwittingly picked up her cue.

"How about the black net? It's sweetly pretty."

Miss Edwards, seeing a chance to get away quickly, agreed at once.

"Oh, yes, it's a duck. You remember it, Mrs. Renton. We copied it I don't know how many times."

"Do I?" Moira looked puzzled. "Would you be an angel, Miss Edwards, and fetch it?"

Miss Edwards went. She knew exactly where the black dress should hang. She put on the light in the evening-dress cupboard. With a disgusted click of her tongue against her teeth she noticed it was not in its place. How tiresome! Why couldn't the girls put the things back on the hangers they took them off? Patiently she started at the end of the line. Each frock was in a sheeting cover. She raised the corner so that she could see what was inside. At the end of the row she shut the cupboard. There was a worried frown on her face. The dress wasn't there. That meant one of the girls had borrowed it. That meant the sack for somebody. "What ill-luck," she thought kind-heartedly, "for that somebody! Of course it was very wrong to borrow things from the shop. All the same, the sack!"

Moira watched her come back with a well-acted look of surprise. Miss Edwards knew it was no good beating about the bush.

"It's not there," she said. "I'm afraid somebody has borrowed it."

"Oh, dear!" Moira frowned. "I did hope we had put a stop to that. From the moment we made the rule that any girl caught doing it had to go, it seemed to cure them."

Miss Edwards nodded.

"So it did too."

Moira got up.

"Well, I needn't keep you. We'll drop the question of my friend's frock for to-night." She turned to Miss Jones. "See Mrs. Brown and tell her the doors are to be locked until you arrive. You had better be here half an hour early. Then put two people you can trust downstairs to open every parcel the girls bring in. Bring the culprit to me."

Although it was absolutely nothing to do with her, nobody could have looked more like a criminal than Pauline when she arrived the next morning. She sidled in at the shop door with the parcel behind her back, looking like a murderer trying to place the body in a trunk in the railway cloak-room. Miss Jones' watchers did not even bother to say, "Can I see what's in that parcel?" But like those who saw the belated entrance of the Jackdaw of Rheims, they exclaimed, "That's him!" And then, because they liked her, they added:

"Oh, Pauline, how could you be such a fool!" and "You idiot, if you were short of a frock why didn't you tell me— I'd have lent you one of mine."

Pauline had rehearsed this horrid entrance mentally all the way from the Cromwell Road. She had seen herself successfully sneaking up the stairs and furtively putting the frock back on its hanger. She had also seen herself caught and heard herself telling of Petronella's crime. The one thing she had not reckoned on was anybody thinking for a moment that she was the culprit.

"But——" she said.

The girls looked at her pityingly.

"Come on, the Jones is waiting for you. You've got to see Mrs. Renton."

"But it——" Pauline began again.

"It's no good saying anything," one of the girls said kindly. "Come on and get it over. It'll all be the same in a hundred years."

Pauline wasted no more time on them, she would explain to Miss Jones. She followed the girls upstairs.

Miss Jones met them on the first floor. Her face grew pink up to the ears when she saw Pauline She spoke in a whisper. Her voice was angry just in the way people sound angry when a child nearly gets run over by a bus.

"Really, Pauline. You! I should never have thought it. Good gracious, child, why couldn't you come to me? You could have bought the dress and had it on account. And now I can't do anything. *She's* here."

"But, Miss Jones," Pauline protested. "You don't understand—it wasn't—"

Miss Jones looked more angry and fussed than ever.

"Excuses only make things worse. Much worse." She went across the passage and knocked on Moira's door. "Here's the girl who took the dress. Most unfortunate." She dropped her voice. "It's one of the twins."

Moira's voice came like a chip falling off a block of ice.

"Send her in."

Pauline, with no time to protest, was pushed by Miss Jones through the door. Surprisingly, Miss Jones, who never showed any affection, gave her arm an encouraging squeeze. Pauline, with the parcel in one hand, stood just inside the room.

Moira, accomplished actress though she was, was too surprised to control herself.

"You!" she exclaimed. Then added, "You never took that dress."

If there was one thing Pauline wanted to hear said it was just that. It's infuriating to be accused of something you haven't done, and infuriating every time you try and explain to be interrupted. But now, when Moira said for her just what she wanted to say she disliked it. She felt as if she had an extra sense, and that extra sense shouted at her, "There's something queer here."

She held out the parcel.

"Here it is."

Moira did not take it. Instead she pointed to a chair. Her voice became suddenly gentle.

"Sit down, my dear."

Pauline obediently sat. Her eyes were fixed on Moira's face. Moira, to her annoyance, found herself looking down at her blotter. Even on the rack she would have denied that Pauline's eyes were too honest for her, but that was the truth.

"I never had a sister," Moira said gently. "I expect it makes a bond I don't understand."

Pauline was always willing to discuss an interesting point.

"Yes, it does. Of course, us being twins makes us particularly tied up."

"Tied up enough to pretend that something one's sister had done was one's own fault?"

Pauline looked at the bit of Moira's face that she could see. It was downcast, the eyes fixed on the blotting-paper on which she was doodling It was difficult with a face at that angle to guess what the person meant exactly, especially a person like Moira, whose intention was mostly expressed by emphasis.

"I suppose one might," she agreed cautiously.

The telephone rang on Moira's desk. It was the house phone. Pauline, without being interested, noticed it was Violet speaking. Her voice was indistinct, disguised by that rattle which queerly seems to get attached to voices when away from the ear to which the telephone is being held. She tried to shut out what was being said, but it was of course impossible.

"I'm awfully sorry, Mrs. Renton." Violet's voice was worried. "She did take it, honestly, I—"

"That's quite all right," said Moira. "I'm busy now. I'll talk to you later." She put down the receiver.

"I'm awfully sorry, Mrs. Renton, she did take it." Pauline was not a suspicious person. But from the moment Moira had said, "You never took it," she had known there was something wrong. Why did Moira know she had never taken it? Now the answer came with horrid distinctness. She knew because she had been told before that it was Petronella. From the sound of Violet's apologies she more than knew, she'd arranged it. Why? The answer to that was obvious. She wanted Petronella dismissed. At this point

132

Pauline's mind slipped back to the day they had arrived. The expression she had caught on Moira's face. The hateful way she had looked at Petronella, the possessive way at David. So that was it. She was jealous. She wanted to marry David herself.

Pauline was quite embarrassed. She felt as though she was taking part in a film instead of being a real person. Real people in the world she had always known didn't scheme like that. It was hateful and despicable, and she wasn't going to let Moira get away with it. It was very hard when the person you were fond of was fond of somebody else. Nobody knew that better than she did. But you couldn't go sneaking about trying to get them dismissed to get them out of the way. They all thought downstairs that she had taken the frock. Then they could go on thinking so.

"We were talking about sisters," Moira was saying. "I have a suspicion that you are shielding that naughty Peter. That's right, isn't it?"

Pauline hated to lie, but after all she was not so much shielding Petronella as scotching Moira's plans.

"No."

Moira tried not to look annoyed, but really she was not going to stand for this stupid girl messing things up.

"My dear," she said gravely. "You mustn't look on me as your manageress but as a friend. However fond you are of your sister, you have yourself to think of. A girl like Peter can easily get another model job, in fact, perhaps I'll help. But it's not so easy for you."

Pauline looked at her with round, interested eyes.

"No, not nearly so easy for me."

"My good child," Moira's voice had a ring of annoyance,

133

"I'm trying to be your friend, but my patience isn't inexhaustible. Now, come along, be sensible. I know exactly what's happened. Peter took the frock. Then this morning she was too scared to bring it back, so you said you would. That's right, isn't it?"

"No."

Moira gave up.

"Are you sticking to this story that you took it, even though you know that I know you never did?"

"Yes."

"Very well." It was a relief to Moira to drop the elder sister tone. "Then you're dismissed. Go to Miss Jones now. She'll pay you what's owing."

Somehow Pauline had never quite seen it was coming to this. Being dismissed is a depressing thing to happen to anyone. It's particularly depressing when it happens to a person whose happiness is dependent on being under the same roof as somebody else. There was a lump in her throat as she got up, but she was not giving Moira the pleasure of seeing that. She couldn't quite manage a smile, but she did succeed in saying "Good-bye".

Moira did not answer the good-bye. Instead she nodded at the parcel which was still in Pauline's hand.

"Put that down. We don't want to lose it altogether. If you have a parcel to take out, I shall give orders it's to be opened before you go."

Pauline turned scarlet. She turned on Moira.

"That's an awfully mean thing to say. It's more than hitting a person who's down, it's kicking them. And you ought to be ashamed of yourself." She planted the parcel on Moira's desk. "Because a person borrows something it doesn't mean they steal."

Moira Belton's blood quivered at being spoken to like that.

"I think you forget who you're speaking to."

"No, I don't." Pauline went to the door. "I'm speaking to Mr. Bliss's manageress and as I'm leaving I can say what I like."

She went out.

In the passage all the temper ran out of Pauline. She had been so angry that she had completely let herself go. The aftermath was chattering teeth and a weak feeling in the knees. She went towards the stairs hardly thinking; just the fact that she was to go to Miss Jones had stuck in her head and guided her feet. Then she came level with David's door and there she stopped.

What had she done? It was all very well to have taken Petronella's sins on her, but she would have liked to put it right with David. Whatever would he think when he heard? If he knew Petronella had borrowed a frock would he mind dreadfully? She didn't think he would. Everybody except Moira, and perhaps Miss Blane, treated Petronella as if she were a precocious ten-year-old and not responsible for her actions. All the same she couldn't tell him. After all, a shop rule was a shop rule. If somebody had to be dismissed for borrowing clothes, then obviously one of them had to go. And of course he would rather it was her than Petronella. She couldn't even get him to buy a tell. He was an honest sort of person and would never let her be punished for something she hadn't done. But it was hard. He had been so nice. All those plans they had made for helping everybody in the autumn. She hated him to believe she would do a mean thing like borrow one of his frocks.

She moved on again. It was no good staring at his door. She had better get her money and go home. Hanging about wasn't making it any easier. She turned at the end of the passage and began to climb the stairs.

"Hullo, Twin." She swung round at the sound of David's voice.

He had evidently just arrived. He was going up to his office. He looked, she thought, so awfully nice that the idea of leaving his shop was more than she could bear. A sob which she swallowed escaped. It burst out like a very large hiccup. Horrified, she put both hands over her mouth.

"Sorry," she gulped. "I must have eaten my breakfast too quickly."

David came up the stairs. He caught hold of her hand.

"That wasn't a hiccup. You're crying. What's up?"

His voice was deliberately gentle, and then he had his hand on hers; the combination broke Pauline. She turned to him with tears streaming down her cheeks.

"I've been sacked."

"What!" He stared at her. "Why? There must be a muddle."

"No." Pauline sniffed, fumbling wildly for her handkerchief. "That's the awful part."

David took his handkerchief out of his pocket.

"Have mine." Pauline mopped her face. "Come to my office and let's hear all about it."

In his office he sat on the edge of his desk. He pulled out a chair for Pauline but she was crying too much to notice.

"Now," he said.

"Well," Pauline gulped. "You see, you have to be

dismissed if you borrow a frock."

"Yes." He agreed. "Moira made that rule."

Pauline played with the handkerchief.

"The black net dress was borrowed last night."

"By you?"

She looked up.

"I was caught sneaking in with the parcel this morning."

She was playing with the handkerchief or she'd have seen a very tender expression on his face. He got up and came to her. He took hold of her chin.

"What's this big act for?"

She sighed. Surely he wasn't going to refuse to believe her too. Why should he?

"What d'you mean?"

"Well, my sweet, the story doesn't ring true. You shouldn't have those truculently honest eyes if you mean to lie. And you shouldn't confide in me that you are going to buy an evening dress when you've saved enough if you are going to pretend that you've borrowed one. Where's Peter?"

"At home being sick."

"Ah!" He put his arm round her. "Now I see. Is she really ill?"

"Only champagne and iced pudding."

"I'll go round and see whether she needs doctoring."

"I'll come with you when I've got my money from Miss Jones."

He took the handkerchief from her and rubbed her cheeks.

"Never cry in London, not if it's ever so. Tears come out black. And stop talking rot about dismissal and Miss Jones."

137

"Oh!" Pauline caught hold of him. "But one of us has to go. It's a rule. And I've said it's me and I'd rather stick to it."

"I suppose the spirit that made people insist on dying on stakes has never departed. On this occasion there's no need for martyrs. The shop is mine and nobody is going to be dismissed."

"Mrs. Renton will be very angry with you."

"I'm not afraid of Moira."

"I am." She rubbed up the pile of the carpet with her toe. "If nobody is going to be dismissed do you mind letting me go on saying it was me?"

"What on earth for?"

Pauline hesitated.

"I wonder if you'll understand."

"Try me."

"When I came this morning I hadn't meant to say it was me. I only did because I found somebody had sneaked to Mrs. Renton."

"Who?"

"I can't tell you that. But they had. They rang her up on the house phone while I was there. They were going to apologize for the muddle of me bringing back the frock. Only as I was there she stopped them."

David looked puzzled.

"Come and sit down." He went over to his desk and pointed to a chair. "Have I got this right? You mean Moira knew?"

"Yes."

David fiddled about in silence with some papers.

He scowled down at them oblivious of Pauline. At last he

looked up.

"Will you ask Violet to come in here?"

Pauline was distressed.

"Now look here, you shouldn't guess. Daddy says it's awfully wrong."

He grinned at her.

"Hop it, Paul."

"But—"

"Hop it. There are more things in heaven and earth, my child, than are dreamed of in your philosophy."

Pauline went to the door, then she turned.

"Did you know you'd said that to me before, or nearly that?"

He laughed.

"I didn't exactly invent it. When did I say it?"

Pauline leant against the door.

"It was the day we first met. Not in church when I was eight. But really met. That Sunday at your aunt's. I'd just said I was afraid I'd not be much use in your shop and you said 'There are more uses for a twin than are dreamed of in your philosophy'."

David's eyes slid in the direction of Moira's room. His lips were grim.

"Did I? Well, I'd almost second sight as it turns out."

CHAPTER 8

"COME IN, VIOLET." Had Pauline heard the tone in which David spoke she would have been amazed. An amused, teasing voice she knew well. An interested voice. Once in a way a tender note. She did not know him when he was disliking somebody. "I want to get this net frock business clear. I hear one of the Lane twins borrowed it. Which?"

Violet was up a tree. What exactly had Mrs. Renton said? The news that Pauline had returned the frock had of course reached the models' room. The news that she was apparently accepting the blame had also reached her. It was that had sent her flying to the telephone. After all, she had been given a rise to persuade Petronella into borrowing it. It would be sickening luck if she were blamed for the muddle and lost the rise. She had not, as a matter of fact, seen Petronella take it. What a mess if it had been Pauline. Suddenly an idea came to her. This would be a chance to straighten things out and get in better than ever with Mrs. Renton. She looked coy.

"Oh, I couldn't tell tales."

"You may as well," David said dryly. "After all, it's no good the wrong one getting blamed."

"Well, I do see that." Violet tried to look as if she were considering. "I suppose really it is a bit unfair if you put it that way. Well, it was Peter."

David's voice was deceptionally casual. He seemed to be thinking of nothing but the paper-knife he was balancing on the ink-pot.

"How d'you know?"

"She told me she was going to take it."

"What did you say?"

Violet looked smug.

"I said it was very wrong of her and she'd get dismissed if she were found out."

"Then you went to Mrs. Renton." It wasn't a question, it was a statement.

Violet turned red. Oh, dear, why hadn't she had a word with Mrs. Renton? Whatever had she said to him?

"Yes," she agreed faintly.

"And Mrs. Renton explained to you why she thought it better to let her take it and get punished."

Violet was completely nonplussed. Whatever had come over Mrs. Renton telling him a thing like that? After all, it wasn't as if it was just any of them, it was Petronella, whom everybody knew he was crazy about.

"I don't know what you mean," she said sulkily.

He looked up.

"I'm paying you a fortnight's salary. You're dismissed."

Violet gasped.

"Whatever for?"

"Because I don't like underhand dealings in my shop."

Violet's eyes narrowed.

"That's a nice way to go on. Who suggested the idea? If your manageress comes to you and asks you to do something for her, what are you going to do? She said I was to tell Peter to take a frock. I never thought of it. Why should I?"

David nodded.

"That's why you're having a fortnight's salary." He gave her a gesture of dismissal. "Next time you get a job don't let people get the idea you're the sort of girl who can be used for rather underhand work. It never pays." He scribbled a note. "Take that up to Miss Jones. She'll give you your money, then you can go at once."

Violet snatched the note.

"All right. But it's a dirty trick. If you want to make trouble, why not make it for those that start it?"

David nodded.

"Don't worry. I will."

His interview with Moira was short. He was on his way to see Petronella. He walked into Moira's office.

"I've dismissed Violet. She's always been a sufficiently nasty bit of work, I don't know why you wanted to push the kid down the drain a bit farther."

Moira managed not to show how her heart was thumping. She looked up. Her voice was bored.

"I thought I had the dismissing of the staff."

"Yes, but not the engineering of it. As you so tactfully arranged that Peter should borrow one of the firm's frocks, beyond a cursing from me she'll hear no more about it. The child's been over gay and her inside's upset. I'll lay her off for a week. The rest in the Vicarage will serve a double purpose of improving her health and punishing her."

"Are you laying yourself off too?"

"Probably." David leant on her desk. "You can be a cad, can't you, Moira? Of all the despicable ways of going on you've about won the prize. I shouldn't do it again, or I'll have to make a change here."

Moira watched him go out without saying a word. Then she picked up the receiver.

"Is that you, Miss Jones? Send out for a bottle of brandy.

142

And if they don't bring it damn quick somebody will get murdered."

Catherine and Pauline were walking round the garden.

"You and Daddy haven't had a holiday this year," said Pauline, stopping to examine a dahlia.

"No." Catherine looked at the dahlia. "Lovely, isn't it? She gave the yellow petals an affectionate pat. "Daddy won't go."

"Because of us?"

Catherine stooped and pulled up a bit of groundsel.

"Not because of you. Daddy is a little worried about Petronella. He says he doesn't think her mind is on the things that really matter."

"It's on the same things it's always been on."

"I know, darling. But fathers are like that. They think anything in their daughters they don't care about must have been picked up outside their homes."

Pauline sighed.

"I wish the summer wasn't nearly over. All these asters and dahlias look like autumn."

"I'm afraid you've not had much summer this year. It must be very stuffy in that shop."

Pauline looked surprised.

"But it's awful fun. I never find it stuffy."

"You've looked very pale sometimes when you've come down at the week-end. And I thought Petronella looked simply wretched when she came home this week. I'm glad Mr. Bliss said she was to have a week's holiday. I wanted to send for the doctor, but she wouldn't let me. She said it was nothing."

Pauline's eyes twinkled behind Catherine's back.

"It was only a bilious attack. She had been dancing rather late."

"Do you go out much?" Catherine asked. Her voice was worried.

"Quite a lot."

"Who introduced you to all these friends?"

"Oh, all sorts of people. We're quite all right, you know."

"I'm sure you are, darling, but I do wish I was there to keep an eye on Petronella. It would be so dreadful if anything happened to her."

"What sort of thing?"

"Well, marrying the wrong man. You read terrible stories in the paper."

Pauline picked a rose.

"Would you be glad if she got married? I mean to someone nice, of course."

Catherine stopped and sniffed at the rose.

"Lovely, isn't it? It's got a nice, old-fashioned smell. Yes, of course I'd be glad. Why, is there anybody?"

Pauline hesitated. She hated to think her mother was worrying, but on the other hand, would David mind? She decided he wouldn't.

"David Bliss is awfully fond of her."

Catherine had been stooping to snip off a dead rose head. She stood upright.

"Is he? Well, of course, that would be splendid, wouldn't it?"

Pauline managed to sound fairly enthusiastic.

"Yes."

"Is she fond of him?"

144

Pauline shrugged her shoulders.

"I don't know. She doesn't show it."

Catherine cut off another dead head.

"I expect that's because she's so young. I suppose I ought to have a talk with her."

"I wouldn't. She'll only laugh. And you know we know all the things you're supposed to tell us!"

"Do you?" Catherine looked relieved. "Mr. Bliss is coming down to-morrow. He's going to stay until Wednesday. Do you think he can be coming because of Petronella?"

Pauline felt suddenly tired. It was very depressing to hear David would be away from the shop for three days. It was particularly depressing just now, for she knew Moira must be loathing her. She had not said a word, but the chances were she would when David was not there to stand up for her. It was frightening to think of those three days. Would Petronella ring up and say she was engaged?

"I should think it's sure to be because of her." She turned towards the house. "I want to unpack. I think I'll go in."

In bed that night Pauline couldn't sleep. Somehow having told her mother about David seemed practically to marry Petronella to him. Lying awake staring dismally into the night, she went through the entire wedding day. How would she be able to bear it? She'd have to be a bridesmaid and look happy. How would she be able to stand in the aisle hearing, "For better for worse, for richer for poorer, in sickness and in health, till death us do part"? And the worst of it would be that she didn't believe Petronella would make him happy. She would most likely say she'd marry him because he designed the sort of clothes she liked

145

wearing, and she was so vague and so good-tempered she never said no to anybody. David, of course, would be terribly happy at first, but he was the sort of person who ought to be loved a lot and Petronella wasn't the sort to ever love anybody a lot. "Oh, goodness," she thought, turning over in bed for the fortieth time, "I wouldn't mind if I thought he'd be happy. But it is mean that somebody who had a stepfather they hated shouldn't be simply terribly happy when they marry They ought to be loved and loved and loved to make up." She dragged the sheet, which had become very hot and twisted, up to her chin. "What will I do if they marry and ask me to stay with them? I couldn't go. I couldn't bear it."

Her surging thoughts grew more depressing as the night went on. She tried to be sensible. "After all," she told herself, "he may not be going to ask her to marry him." But her reason rejected the idea. "Why was he coming? Why should he spend three days in the middle of the week with his aunt unless it was for that?" As the clock struck three she could bear it no more. "It's no good fussing and fussing," she said to herself firmly. "You'd better get some milk and a biscuit and perhaps you'll go to sleep."

The passage outside seemed very black and creaky. She couldn't turn on a light for fear of waking her mother, who was a light sleeper. She fumbled her way to the stairs, found the banister and groped down to the hall. Her father's study was the first door on the left; to her surprise she saw a light under it. She hesitated, wondering if he were still up or had left his light on. As she paused, the door opened and Mark, rubbing his head with weariness, came out. He switched on the passage light and saw Pauline.

"Hullo, my dear. What is it?"

"Aren't you late?" said Pauline, shocked. "Do you know it's after three?"

"Is it? I was working on my sermon and never noticed. Where are you going?"

"I was hungry." She saw how tired he looked. "Would you like some Bovril or something?"

Mark shook his head.

"It's Sunday. I don't like taking anything before Holy Communion."

Pauline forgot her own troubles at seeing him so tired.

"You don't think it wrong, so it isn't wrong for you. I'll boil you some hot milk."

Mark smiled at her.

"Very well. I dare say I shall sleep better."

Pauline led him to the kitchen.

"A fat lot of good sleeping well is going to do you when you write sermons until three and then get up at half-past six for church."

Mark sat wearily at the kitchen table while Pauline got milk and a saucepan.

"I've always found sermons on faith difficult. It seems to me very hard to persuade people to have faith, and to trust God is working His purpose out when there's so much suffering in the world."

Pauline put a match to the gas.

"Do you believe He's always working a purpose out?"

"Of course."

She put the saucepan on the gas.

"A lot of things seem to me unfair."

"That's because you only see a bit of the pattern. If you

147

could see it all—all the threads that make up the warp and woof, you'd understand."

She found a tin of biscuits and put it on the table.

"I don't believe I would. You make everything sound as though God were making a counterpane or something."

"In a way He is."

"Well, if He is, anybody would rather be one of the bits that made flowers and things and not be just background."

The milk boiled. She poured it into two cups and put it on the table. Mark took a biscuit and broke it thoughtfully.

"Would they? You know, Pauline, I couldn't go on being a parson if I wasn't as sure of the law of compensation as I am sure of the love of God."

Pauline put her tongue in her milk to see if it was too hot to drink. It was. She blew on it.

"You mean if one person seems to have everything and another person nothing, that if one saw all the counterpane, things even up?"

Mark didn't answer for a bit. He drank his milk, his tired eyes lit up with his thoughts. Then he nodded.

"Yes. Pain, suffering, heart-break. If we could see all the pattern it's the finest threads that are given the strain."

Pauline finished her milk.

"It would be nicer to be a weak thread," she suggested.

Mark got up.

"Rubbish. Come up to bed." He put his arm round her. "It's a sign of love if you're tried high. And love is the beginning of the law."

Pauline, warmed by milk, settled down in bed again. She was comforted.

"I hope, then, there's a special plan for me," she thought

148

drowsily. And went to sleep.

Moira was having an even worse night than Pauline. She had known when she went to bed she was in for a bad one. She had been late dining and playing poker. She had drunk too much champagne at dinner and too many brandies and sodas after it. It was half-past two when she got in.

The wretched Ida was dosing in a chair. She sprang up at the sound of Moira's latch-key. Moira could carry an almost unlimited supply of drink and not show a sign except to the very experienced eye. Ida had a super-experienced eye where Moira was concerned.

"Oh, dear," she thought. "Tight. That's a nice look-out for to-morrow, and me hoping to get her out early." She said nothing to Moira. Many such evenings had taught her that when Moira had drunk too much, whatever she said was sure to be wrong.

"Here." Moira flung her fox cape and evening bag at her. "For God's sake get a move on."

Ida put the cape and bag on a chair. With great deftness she manceuvred Moira so that her back was to the light. She unhooked her frock.

"Thank you, Madam," she said as it came undone. "If you don't mind." She slipped her hands under the skirt and lifted it over Moira's head. Moira made an impatient movement and a hook caught in her hair.

"Blast you!" She threw her head sideways. "Why can't you look what you're doing?"

"I'm sorry, Madam." Ida disentangled the hook and took off the frock.

"I've had a filthy week," Moira growled as she sat down at her dressing-table. "Then to-night I lost thirty pounds, and now you can't even get my clothes off. What the hell do you think I pay you for?"

"I'm sorry you lost, Madam."

"You can't be as sorry as I am. Hang that up and get out."

Ida hung up the frock and gave a quick look round the room. The coral pink chiffon nightdress lay ready to put on. A coral pink dressing-gown was over the back of a chair with slippers to match under it. The possible drugs Moira might want waiting on the bed table, with a bottle of Vichy Celestins beside them. There was nothing more Moira could possibly require as far as she could see.

"Good night, Madam."

Moira, left alone, finished undressing. Angrily she cleaned her face and slapped on face cream. Angrily she washed and cleaned her teeth.

"Silly idiot," she muttered, "pulling my hair like that. I wouldn't wonder if she did it on purpose."

Over by her bed she stood looking at the collection of medicines.

"My sleeping stuff doesn't work on brandy," she thought. Then she shrugged her shoulders and poured out a double dose. "No harm done in trying."

The effect of the drug on the drinks she had taken was merely sobering. It drove any thought of sleep out of her head, and left her terribly overstrung and nervous. As always, nervous depression fixes on some incident likely to aggravate. Moira's landed on the scene with David.

She went over that morning from the beginning. The row with Pauline, each word David had said, and the more she tore the situation to pieces the more hysterical she became. But even with the after effect of drink and a sleeping-draught working on her highly keyed temperament she had to see and face the facts.

"It's no good getting away from it," she told herself. "You let yourself in badly over that. And what's more, my girl, you aren't sitting so pretty. You refused the partnership, and now you look as if you'd made a proper muddle of the whole damn thing."

She sat up in bed and turned on the light. Half-past four. She picked up the mirror by her bed and looked at her face. It wasn't a good time to do it. Every line that dissipation had given her stood out as if it had been etched.

"My God, you look a hag," she said reflectively, "and," added inquiringly, "so what?"

Propped up in bed at half-past four, Moira took stock of herself. For once she didn't gloss the situation. Tommy Renton's ghost sat on her bed, and with it a good many more. The life she led and meant to go on leading appeared as sordid to her at that moment as it did at all times to others.

"Sooner or later," she thought, "there'll come an end to fun. Those blasted twins have mucked me up properly. Married to David, I'd have been parked. And it's mostly that wretched Paul's fault. What the hell did she want to butt in for? Why couldn't she have let Peter shoulder her own sins? But if she had," she reasoned truthfully, "David would never have sacked the girl."

She lit a cigarette and stared at the coils of smoke.

The question was what to do next. Should she drop the marriage plan and try and get David back to the partnership idea?

"And that won't be so easy," she thought. "He's so touchy

now he's in love. I don't believe I can do a thing until they're both out of the shop. But how?"

At seven o'clock she gave up the idea of sleeping and rang for her tea. Ida struggled up from the depths of sleep and flung on a dressing-gown. The service maid had just arrived to do the flat. She grinned at Ida.

"Been on the tiles?"

Ida scowled.

"Up late waiting for *her,* and now she wants her tea. Seven o'clock. She might remember there's others that like a bit of sleep."

The maid looked sympathetic.

"That's right. Never thinks of us, some of them. How about taking her the Sunday papers. Been a lovely murder down Dover way. That ought to keep her quiet for a bit."

"She's not all that crazy on murders. Afraid of being done in herself, I shouldn't wonder."

"And from all I hear she's one that might be worth hanging for."

Ida picked up the kettle and made the tea.

"You've said it," she agreed sourly.

To distract her thoughts, Moira opened the least truthful of the papers. Idly sipping her tea, she skimmed the sensational and improbable headlines. In the centre of one page was a glaring announcement. She looked at it with no interest. Then suddenly she put down her cup and read it with absorbed attention. When she had finished she lay back and stared at the ceiling.

"Now I shouldn't wonder at all if that was to-day's bright thought."

CHAPTER 9

IT WAS TUESDAY. A warm perfect day. David got up whistling. It was fine and he was taking Petronella for a drive and lunch. He was doing the sensible thing at last, putting an end to all his sleeplessness and restlessness. To-day he'd ask Petronella "What about it?" Last night he had felt nervous at the thought. What would he do if she said "No"? To-day, with the sun shining, he knew she would say "Yes".

His aunt heard him whistling. She was at her dressing-table. On it in a folding frame was a picture of her brother-in-law, David's father. She picked it up. He was in uniform staring straight out of the picture. She nodded to him.

"I don't like it, and you wouldn't have liked it. But you always said let a young horse have his head. Dragging at his mouth only sours him. But I wish it was the other sister. She's just your sort."

Petronella too was delighted to see it was fine. She had planned if it were she would wear a new hat. Catherine was in the hall when she came down dressed.

"Dear me, darling, isn't that a very big hat for motoring?"

"Yes." Petronella examined herself with approval in the hall glass. "But I saw a picture of Ginger Rogers in one like it."

Catherine gave her daughter a puzzled stare. She certainly did look charming. But surely there were occasions when you wanted to be yourself.

"Don't you think Mr. Bliss would rather you looked like

153

Petronella Lane?"

Petronella stared at her mother in amazement. Then she giggled.

"You are funny, Mum. You said that in the soppiest voice."

Catherine flushed. Her voice had sounded a bit sentimental, she'd noticed it herself. But really it was difficult to know what to say to Petronella, and it did seem an occasion when a little sentimentality would not be out of place. She could remember as though it were yesterday the day when Mark had asked her to marry him. It had been so like Mark who never worried about such things that he had led her through the rose garden, down the herbaceous borders, into the kitchen garden, and not till they were surrounded with cabbages did he take her hands and whisper what he had to ask. When she had gone out with him that morning her mother (though she did not really approve the match) had said "Bless you, little daughter." And she had not laughed, she had thought it right that everybody should feel emotional with her. Perhaps Petronella only laughed because she wasn't in love. Catherine was the last person to want anybody to marry unless they were in love, but all the same she thought it would be convenient if Petronella said "Yes". Really somebody looking like she looked ought to have a man to take care of her. However, she was not risking further giggles.

"Take a coat," she said practically, "and do bring him back to tea."

David thought he had never seen anything more beautiful than Petronella standing in the Vicarage door.

She had on a simple white frock copied from one he had designed. The Ginger Rogers hat was white straw trimmed with green velvet ribbons. Her breath-catching legs had on sheer very uncountry sunburnt stockings. She wore white shoes.

"Hullo, poppet." He opened the door for her. "How are you? Strong enough to go back to work to-morrow?"

Petronella wriggled comfortably into her seat.

"You are a beast. I've had an awful time pretending to be ill."

He patted her hand.

"Well, don't let's quarrel. To-day's a holiday. Where'd you like to go?"

"Brighton," said Petronella promptly.

He looked at her in dismay.

"My sweet! Brighton in September. It'll be full of trippers."

"The Metropole'll be all right. And we needn't go out."

He looked gloomy.

"What a picture! Have you ever been to the Metropole?"

"No. But I've always wanted to. All the other models have."

"I don't doubt it. Tell you what, let's lunch at the Metropole and go on somewhere afterwards."

All the way to Brighton Petronella prattled. She talked as usual of film stars, hair-dressing and clothes. David tried now and again to steer the conversation to more personal channels, but Petronella never noticed conversations being steered. What she found interesting she was sure everybody found interesting. At lunch it was obviously impossible to say anything but banalities. But after lunch,

155

when she showed signs of lingering, he took a firm hand.

"Come on, sweet. You're going to see the downs."

Up above Brighton he turned on to a bumpy down road. Then off it to a quiet patch amongst gorse bushes. He looked at the rolling miles of close-bitten brown-yellow turf. He threw open the sunshine roof and took off his hat.

"Isn't this grand?"

Petronella looked distastefully at the view.

"It's just grass."

David turned round and took her hands.

"Do you remember a Sunday when I came to tea with you?"

Petronella opened her eyes. This hand-holding she was quite used to, only it was usually more hand-grabbing. But the next step in her recent experiences was not questions about remembering, it wasn't talking at all, it was violent kisses mixed up with gasps and explosive " you are so lovely" or "I can't help it, I adore you." However, she always wanted to please. She let her mind hover back to the Sunday. At once she remembered.

"Of course. It was the first time I wore my blue dress."

"Your blue dress looked marvellous. But something else happened besides your wearing it. I asked you if you could ever care for me."

"Oh, that!" Petronella stifled a yawn. She didn't want to be rude, but really sitting looking at grass talking about caring for people wasn't her idea of the best way to spend a Sunday.

"It's not 'oh, that' to me," said David, feeling hurt. "I meant it. I love you."

Probably no man can make a statement like that and not

156

expect some reaction. David certainly expected one. But he had not got on to the life Petronella led. Night after night since that first party at the Savoy she was seized in somebody's arms on the way home, and that somebody (shaking and damp) muttered, amongst other things, that he loved her. Saying they loved you was one of the things men did, Petronella supposed, and she generally bore it perfectly calmly unless they got too frenzied and then she would mildly expostulate, "Gosh, you'll tear my frock." Now, since nothing was being torn and she wasn't being crushed, she did not consider there was any reason to say anything. Instead she pointed out a chalk-blue butterfly which was hovering over the car.

"Isn't that a nice colour?"

David caught hold of her shoulders. He almost shook her.

"You are a little beast. Don't you care at all what other people feel?"

Petronella opened her eyes.

"Goodness, you do sound cross. Of course I care. Why?"

"I suppose you haven't listened while I told you I loved you."

"Of course I've listened. Did you want me to say something?"

David shook his head despairingly.

"Oh, no! A man only says things like that for fun."

"That's what I've found." Petronella agreed, very deaf to tones of voice. "After all, everybody says it on the way home, don't they?"

"Do they?" He took his hands off her shoulders and put his arm round her. His voice was amused. "Do you mean to say, duckie, that every man you know says it?"

"Yes." Petronella took off her hat. "If he's going to start hugging," she thought, "I don't want that spoilt."

But David didn't hug. Instead he just held her lightly. She might have been his sister.

"I wonder if you'll ever grow up?"

"I don't know." Petronella put her head on his shoulder. "That's a funny thing. Pauline and I are exactly the same age and she's much more sensible than me."

David had a sudden vision of Pauline's serious little face. She had said, "All my life it's things like Petronella's curls that people remember." Was it possible that Petronella had to be remembered for her loveliness because there was nothing else to remember? He looked down at her almost white curls and incredibly black eyelashes. He stroked her cheek.

"Bored, sweet?"

"Well," said Petronella honestly, "it isn't very exciting here, is it?"

"Would you like to go back to the Metropole?"

She sat up and took her lip-stick from her bag.

"Home, John, and don't spare the horses."

Moira was lunching at a flat in the Albany. Opposite to her, across the table, sat an old man whose beaky nose and snow-white hair were better known to thousands in Fleet Street than the noses and hair of their own fathers. Sir Robert Nilk owned a vast network of papers, known collectively as the Nilk Press. Thanks to these by a mere nod to one of his underlings he could break and make people in a night. And by blazing shock headlines across his paper he could change the opinions of all the gullible in the British Isles.

Amongst Sir Robert's hobbies was a penchant for pretty aristocratic women. Amongst those he had collected was Moira. He had been held by her for quite a time, although his reason told him he was a fool, for she dragged money out of him shamelessly and blatantly. Because she was clever she had never allowed him (even after he had lost interest in her) to go quite out of her life.

Throughout lunch they had a verbal fencing match. Moira wanted to get down to what she had come about. Sir Robert, who hated being bothered during meals, was determined she shouldn't tell him until they reached the coffee. Probably she wanted money and that would mean a distressing scene for he certainly wasn't going to give her any more, and Moira (who knew some sordid facts about him which she brought up in arguments) was extra-ordinarily nasty when crossed.

Sir Robert won. The coffee was served and the man had gone out of the room before Moira said:

"Now look here, I've got to get back. It wasn't only to hear your wit and gaze on your beautiful body that I invited myself to lunch."

Sir Robert cut a cigar.

"So I imagined. Well, what is it?"

She lit a cigarette.

"Do you read your own Sunday rag?"

"I read all my papers. You know that."

"Well, then you know you're running a competition?"

He nodded.

"The loveliest girl in England to be Miss Metropolis at

the newspaper's fair at Christmas."

"That's it." Moira puffed out a mouthful of smoke. "I've got the winner for you."

Sir Robert went on fiddling with his cigar. He did not seem to be attending. In reality (as she well knew) he was sieving her words and arriving at her motive.

"One supposes you mean the child that Bliss is in love with."

Moira gave him an admiring look. She often thought Sir Robert tiresome, but she never failed to enjoy his sharpness of perception.

"Yes. Her name's Petronella Lane."

"I've never seen her. But I hear she's quite beautiful. But however that may be, the competition is fair. I've four judges, honest people. Even you couldn't get them to perjure their souls."

Moira moved impatiently.

"I'm not worrying about that. She'll win all right. After all, how many beauties are there in a generation?"

Sir Robert looked at her curiously.

"It's unlike you, my dear, to sing the praises of one of your own sex."

Moira shrugged her shoulders.

"I'm not a fool. I know beauty when I see it."

"If that is so, where do I come in? If this girl is bound to win, which you obviously wish, how is my help needed?"

Moira tapped the ash off her cigarette. Here was the crux of the interview. She leant forward in her chair.

"I want you to add to the prize. Could you guarantee that an American film company gave the winner a test?"

Sir Robert's eyes twinkled

"How like you, Moira my dear. What a long chance to get rid of an unwanted young woman."

"I believe in long chances. Could you arrange it?"

"Yes. But how do you know an English company won't sign her up first? After all, as an entrant for the competition her picture will be published."

Moira laughed.

"Her picture's been published for weeks wearing our clothes. Did you ever know an English film company who looked for new faces? They never know we have any till they're signed up for Hollywood. Besides, that's the other thing I came about. I don't want her picture published as an entrant."

Sir Robert looked at her sharply.

"The lady in question is under age. She is the daughter of a parson called Lane who would certainly object to his daughter being a competitor in a beauty competition. Bliss would come down to Fleet Street and ring my neck if I dared to say she was an entrant. All of which I suppose means that you are sending in the photograph?"

Moira's eyes twinkled

"I must say asking you favours saves one a whole lot of talking. Yes. Not that I couldn't get the girl to agree, she'll like the idea. But I think I won't tell her till it's time for the final judging."

"And when I've arranged with the American film company, and given orders the picture is not to be reproduced, what do I get out of it?"

"The find of a century. If you don't see a way of making money out of that, you've changed a lot."

He chuckled.

"You're a clever woman, my dear. All right. See the photograph comes to me personally. And, Moira," he caught her hand as she got up to go, "if you bring it off and manage to pack the little creature off to Hollywood, and then manage to marry Bliss, don't tell him my share. He might murder me. I can't think of a more terrifying fate than to be married to you."

Not knowing of Moira's schemes, Pauline was puzzled at her good temper. Overtired from lack of sleep, hollow-eyed from worrying, she made a bad mistake in the showroom. Half the staff were away on their summer holidays and she was put on to attend to the customers. On the Tuesday, while David was motoring Petronella to Brighton, she was showing tweeds to Lady Done. As she flipped over the pattern book her mind was not on what she was doing. It was in the country watching Petronella's face, wondering what she was saying, if it were happening now.

"I think that's charming," said Lady Done. "How much would the model cost copied in this?"

The list of prices was lying on a desk. Pauline went over and looked at it. The list said thirty-five pounds quite clearly, but somehow in her distressed state she read it as twenty-five. Lady Done was delighted. She said they could get on with it at once and went out.

"What did she want?" said Ann, the girl who was head of the showroom while Miss Edwards was away.

"The new *tailleur*. It's to be made in this." Pauline showed the pattern.

"Ought to look nice. I'm surprised she took the price quietly. She generally tries to beat us down. Thirty-five's more than she usually goes to."

"Thirty-five!" Pauline turned crimson. "My goodness, I told her twenty-five."

"You didn't!" Horror-struck the two stared at each other.

"Could I telephone?" Pauline suggested. Ann nodded.

"You'd better. She won't be in yet. Leave a message. And then write."

Pauline phoned. She heard the bell ring and a voice say "Hullo". Then with a sick feeling she heard "No. Her Ladyship is staying in the country. No. She said not to send any letters. She'd be back on Monday."

"That's done it, must be up for the day," said Ann. "You'll have to go and tell *her*."

Pauline swallowed.

"Must I?"

Ann nodded.

"Afraid so. Better go at once and get it over."

That was when Pauline was so surprised. If anything was certain it was that Moira would be furious. She expected to be given notice almost before she explained what she had done. But Moira, hot on her new scheme, had no intention of alienating David with any more attacks on the twins. She was furious about the tweed because at that price she lost her own rake off. Thirty was the price she and David had decided on. At twenty-five there was five pounds loss to the firm, and not a cent could be screwed off it, but she managed to keep her rage to herself.

"It was very careless, my dear," she said coldly. "You must keep your mind on what you're doing. However, it can't be helped now."

Pauline, wide-eyed, recounted this conversation to a startled Ann.

"Really she was quite nice."

Ann was sceptical.

"When she's nice I'm most nervous. It's not the sort of thing she's ever nice about. You mark my words. There's something up."

But Pauline was doubtful. Was her father right? Were there nice things about everybody if you looked?

"I expect," she thought, "I've just been mean and looking for her faults. After this I'll think whatever she does, she means to be nice really."

It was with a singing heart that Pauline came to the shop the next morning. There had been no telephone message and there surely would have been if Petronella were engaged. And David was coming back that day. Of course he was motoring Petronella up, and all that time in a car he might say anything; but the shop seemed so incredibly dreary when he was not in it, that so long as he came back she did not mind how.

It was about twelve o'clock that she ran into him. He looked ill.

"Hullo, Twin," he said cheerfully, but her ear detected a falsity in the note. "How's things?"

"Oh, goodness, haven't you heard? I've lost you money. I sold Lady Done a dress at the wrong price. She's having the new *tailleur.* She's having it made in one of those tweeds that you get from that place in Leeds. She said 'How much?' and I went and looked, and would you believe it, even looking I said the wrong price. I must have seen it said thirty-five, but I said twenty-five. Wasn't I a fool?"

David was tired and depressed, but something in the story struck him as odd, though he couldn't at the moment

164

bother what it was.

"Thirty-five!" he repeated vaguely.

"Yes. I told Mrs. Renton. She was awfully nice about it."

"Moira was!" This time he was frankly amazed. "You must have got her at a very forgiving moment! I'm going away for a holiday, Twin."

"No!" Pauline was so upset she spoke before she had time to guard her voice. "Are you? Why?"

"I'm going to play cricket."

"But you weren't last week. You said you didn't know when you'd go away."

He smiled at her with amusement.

"Don't be angry with me. I can change my mind." He looked down the corridor as if it were a limitless lane. "I thought it was time I got away. I think perhaps my eye's getting out."

"What for, designing?"

"For that and other things too." He caught her arm. "I'll be back at the beginning of next month and then we'll dine together, and you can tell me what I'm to do for my workpeople. Is that a bargain?"

Pauline tried to smile, but the beginning of next month felt aeons away.

"Yes. I'll have my new frock by then."

Pauline puzzled about David all day. "He looks," she thought, "sort of miserable. He looks like somebody who couldn't have what they wanted. Could Petronella have said she wouldn't marry him? "But as she bustled about with her hands full of patterns and snippets of silk she rejected the idea. Never in her life had Petronella done anything pointblank so to speak. She might have said she

165

wasn't sure, but Pauline could not believe she had gone further. She left sounding her until they were home. It would be hopeless asking her on the way back from work. She would be sure to go on discussing it in the bus, quite likely mentioning David's name so that everybody knew who they were talking about.

She was rather hindered by Miss Williams. Petronella was of course going out, and Miss Williams had to come in to take a look at her pet.

"Green frock is all nice-ums again. 'Ou must be careful. Poor, poor Aunty-mum took two hours stitching at torn frockums."

"Gosh," said Petronella, "I wish I was rich. I'm tired of my clothes."

Miss Williams smoothed out the skirts of the green frock which was on the bed.

"It's a p'itty, p'itty f'ock."

"The frock's all right," Petronella agreed. "It's only I've worn it so often."

Miss Williams was at the door. She turned with a coy look.

"I know somebody who's got a lot of gentlemen who 'oves them terwibly."

Pauline looked disgustedly after Miss Williams.

"I can't think how you can bear her."

Petronella, without a stitch on, was sitting on her bed putting on her stockings. She looked up.

"I don't care what anybody says as long as they're useful."

Pauline went over to the dressing-table. She picked up the comb and fiddled with its teeth.

"Was it nice at home?"

"Of course it wasn't. I was awfully bored, and Mum said she thought I needed something to do and made me address two hundred envelopes about a jumble sale. I thought it was mean, as I'd been ill."

"But you hadn't."

"She didn't know that."

Pauline ran her finger along the top of the teeth of the comb.

"Did you have fun with David?"

Petronella put on some knickers.

"Part of it was all right. We went to lunch at the Metropole at Brighton. I've always wanted to go there. But afterwards he went all rural."

"How?"

"Drove his car on to the downs to look at the view. I hate views."

Pauline saw the scene clearly and painfully.

"Didn't he want to talk?"

Petronella joined her at the dressing-table and put powder on her nose.

"No. Men don't in cars. It's just mutter, mutter, hug."

Pauline turned away and sat on her bed. There was something missing in the story, she was sure. David wasn't the sort of man just to want to mutter and hug. He was in love with Petronella. Why hadn't he asked her to marry him? But he hadn't. That was the fact that stuck out clearly and sent her heart bounding. It was ridiculous to be pleased. She knew from the bottom of her soul that his not being fond of Petronella would never make him throw a glance in her direction. All the same, however silly it was of her, she couldn't help being glad. Nothing would be so bad as it really happening.

September was a hard-working and depressing month for both twins. The departure of Violet had made it urgent that Petronella should become a showroom model. Up to date she had been the inspiration of most of David's débutante designs, and the first photographic model. Now the other three were put on to teach her showroom work, and very stupid they found her. She had not the faintest idea why a dress was good. It meant nothing to her that pockets had a new line, that coats were reversible, that an idea with initials was amusing. She just looked in the glass, saw she looked nice, and perhaps reminiscent of a pet film star, and, quite satisfied, wandered vaguely into the showroom, smiling blandly, and stood about. But her inability to see the finer points in the dresses was not her worst fault. It was her looks.

Miss Edwards (back from her walking-tour holiday, which had proved one long argument, for Tom hated her to pay for everything) was driven nearly mad. She would have a rich mother in the showroom with a plain daughter. Miss Edwards did her patter perfectly.

"I quite understand. I've just the frock for her. Very sympathetic to the angles of young girls, and at the same time young." Then she would turn to one of her assistants. "Tell Peter to show the white and green."

A few minutes later Peter would stroll casually into the showroom. From the doorway her beauty gave the effect of light coming into a dark room. She smiled vaguely at Miss Edwards, the mother, daughter and anybody who happened to be about.

Now if there was one type which did not feel an irresistible urge to stroke and pet Petronella, it was the mothers of plain, rather-difficult-to-marry-off daughters. Those mothers sniffed and started at once to run down the clothes, subtly suggesting the fault was Petronella's.

"Quite nice. But rather showy."

"That is seeing it in this light," Miss Edwards suggested, hurriedly turning Petronella round so that her radiant face was out of view. "You see how charmingly young-girl that sash is."

"Well, the back is rather nice," the mother would agree, cheered by a back not so different from her own daughter's. "Perhaps——"

Then Petronella would spoil it all by looking round.

"Oh, I'm so sorry, Miss Edwards, I've forgotten the flowers." She would turn in a friendly way to the customers. "There's some flowers for the belt."

That finished it. The sight of Petronella (who could not move into an unbecoming position) stooping to show where exactly the flowers would go, was too much for the mother.

"No. Really that is too showy. Let me see something simpler."

"Shall I put on the pink?" Petronella would suggest. She then smiled at the girl. "I saw a photograph of Olivia de Haviland in one like it."

The girl would sit up and look hopeful.

"And who," inquired the mother, "is Miss de Haviland?"

The girl and Petronella would exchange glances which put all people in the grown-up class completely beyond the pale.

"A film star, Mother."

Miss Edwards hurriedly would push Petronella out of the room.

"Tell Betty to wear the pink, or, if she is not there, Mary can. Whatever happens, I don't want you to show it."

September was hot. Eloise, Mary and Betty were fond of Petronella, but they did have days when they thought they were being unfairly treated.

"You don't try, Petronella," Eloise complained. "You're never allowed to show more than one frock to a customer."

"And me," said Mary, "who this very day has shown sixteen frocks to that wretched Lady Sybil Luptern and she's not bought one. I'd like to see you showing sixteen frocks to anybody."

"I can't think what Petronella does in the showroom," Betty complained. "She's no sooner in than she's out, and one of us is told off to show the rest to her customer. And nobody seems to blame her. That's what gets me."

It was Miss Edwards in bed one night who solved the problem of what to do with Petronella. It came to her in an enlightened flash. "Brides!" The mothers of girls already safely engaged and already at the trousseau stage feared nobody, however good-looking. "But," she added, as a mental reservation, "she shan't come into the showroom if the fiancés are there. That's asking for trouble."

Pauline, living from day to day with that blank feeling anyone is bound to have when the only person who matters is away, carried dutifully on with her work. She lacked all interest, but succeeded in being efficient and giving an impression of somebody who was busy and interested. After her lapse over the tweed dress she was careful not to let her mind woolgather in work hours. It was David's shop, she mustn't let him down.

Moira sent Sir Robert the loveliest of Petronella's photographs. There were masses to choose from, as there was practically no style of garment in which she had not posed. With unerring instinct she selected one posed to show a new collar. She was looking full face at the lens. All her incredible features, the width between her eyes, the odd enhancing gleam lighting her nose, the perfect mouth, and the delicious way her hair grew, were all there for the discerning eye to see. The perfection of her figure, and her quite perfect legs, could wait to startle the judges when they saw her in the flesh.

Sir Robert acknowledged the picture in a scrawl in his own handwriting :

This is the face that launched a thousand ships. Though I remember Langtry, and have seen all our modern, much-publicized beauties, there has been nothing like it. Be careful of her. Such beauty is a gift from the gods and their vengeance will fall on you if you hurt what could only have been moulded on Olympus.

In the first week in October, just when Pauline was beginning to get a faint colour in her cheeks because soon David must be back, the worst trouble fell on "Reboux" that they had ever known. Every dressmaking business has its crises, but this one so far exceeded every other crisis they had ever dreamt of in nightmares, that afterwards it was always spoken of as "the Pulford muddle". And the worst of it was that everybody was more or less to blame, especially

171

Pauline.

The Pulfords had one daughter. The same one that squinted for whom David had gone to Scotland to design a dress. The Pulfords were one of the last surviving bit of British aristocracy who believed God had designed three classes. Royalty, of whom the sons might marry into their family. Their family, and a very limited set of friends of theirs. And others. Their daughter (known to half England as the Pulford hag), whose real name was the Lady May Alexandra Victoria de Porville Pulford, had been graced by heaven with neither looks nor any semblance of brains. But she was good. And being good, had taken the eye of an equally good first cousin who, since he could pass few exams, had been pushed into the Church in order that he might fall comfortably into a family living.

The Pulfords being famous, the wedding was to be a big affair with royalty present. It was being held at a castle they owned in Warwickshire. But it happened that one week before the wedding a kitchen-maid at the castle got scarlet fever, and the local doctor, who cared more for germs than aristocracy, put all the servants into quarantine and ordered the castle to be fumigated. The Pulfords roared with rage, but they couldn't fight the medical profession, so at the eleventh hour all the invitations went out again stating that the wedding would be held at The Priory, the Pulford home in Sussex.

Naturally, "Reboux's" were told of the change, since it was their business, the day before the wedding, to deliver the bride's, twelve bridesmaids' and two pages' clothes. Miss Jones received the message, and gave it to Miss Edwards, who gave it to her assistants, who sent Pauline with it up to Miss Blane, who in due course told Miss Maud, and Miss Maud told the packing-room. Yet somehow, when the moment came to dispatch the clothes, they went to the castle in Warwickshire.

Early the next morning the first news of disaster arrived. The Duchess of Pulford's personal maid rang up at nine from Sussex. The six o'clock train had been met last night as arranged and where were the clothes?

Off went Miss Jones flying scared from department to department. Everybody swore they had either given the right message or had not been given it to give. But the packing-room were quite definite. Two girls in two taxis had taken the boxes to the station and seen them off by the passenger train due at six-two. Each box clearly labelled to the castle in Warwickshire.

Everybody lost their heads. The telephone pealed unceasingly. The Duchess rang up and almost froze the wire in her rage. The Duke rang up and nearly burnt it with his blasphemies. Every bridesmaid's mother phoned and pleaded or scolded. The pages' mothers phoned and cried. To each and all Miss Jones, sounding less and less reliable, said, "Yes, your grace," or "Yes, m'lady. They'll be there in time."

Meanwhile Miss Blane and Miss Edwards on the other telephone wildly rang up the station in Warwickshire. They found the boxes were there, but no train leaving in time to get them to Sussex for a wedding at two-thirty.

In the middle of the fuss Miss Maud, red-eyed with crying, met Pauline on the stairs.

"The packing-room say they never had the message," she sobbed. "I'm sure I gave it to them. It was written down

173

just as Miss Blane gave it to me. When Mrs. Renton comes it's sure to mean the sack."

"Well, Miss Blane had the message right," Pauline said firmly. "I took it to them. The wedding was at a castle instead of a priory."

Miss Edwards' eyes rounded like saucers.

"You didn't say that, did you? It's the other way round."

Pauline looked harassed.

"Goodness! I don't remember. I just took a message. I'm sure I gave the one that was given to me."

Nobody could help admiring Moira when she arrived. She wasted no time on asking who had done what. She looked at her staff with scorn.

"Ring up Croydon and tell them I want an aeroplane. Tell them where the place is in Warwickshire, and tell them to arrange to have a car waiting at the nearest landing-ground." She picked up the telephone receiver.

"Hullo. No, I'd like to speak to the Duchess herself." There was a pause. "Hullo. Moira Renton speaking. The things are coming by plane. All right, I'll bring my head fitter. No, don't worry, they'll be there hours before anybody has to dress."

Pauline spent the rest of the morning behaving like Alice. Only instead of saying, "Do cats eat rats?" she kept muttering, "The wedding will now be held at The Priory, Pulford St. Annes, Sussex." And alternatively, "The wedding will now be held at The Castle, Warwickshire." Either way it sounded wrong. She was not made less confused by the rest of the staff, who, though they were fond of her, were thankful to find a scapegoat, and looked at her as if she had proved to be a poisoner.

It was nearly one when the telephone rang, and a faint voice said:

"Miss Blane speaking from The Priory. All the clothes are here. No, terrible. I was air sick the whole way, and Mrs. Renton was most displeased."

With the relief of good news everybody felt hungry. One o'clock was not an hour when customers often came in.

"Somebody must stay in the showroom," said Miss Edwards. She looked at Pauline. "Will you?"

"Oh, please I'd like to," Pauline agreed humbly.

The girls streamed out chattering. Nobody said so, but it was clearly understood that if they took a minute or two extra over their lunch, and it came off Pauline's time, it was the least she could expect after the morning she had given them.

Left alone, Pauline stretched back absolutely exhausted in a chair. She felt quite hysterical. So hysterical that suddenly in her relief she began to cry.

"My dear Twin! What's the matter?"

She didn't need to look up. She would have known that voice anywhere.

"You!" Then she did a thing which on looking back very much surprised her. She flung herself into David's arms. "Oh, goodness," she sobbed, "I am glad to see you. The Pulford clothes went where the kitchen-maid has scarlet fever and the marriage isn't. And everybody thinks it's me."

David held her away from him.

"Pull yourself together one second, ducky. Do you mean to say that all the things for the Pulford hag's nuptials are in Warwickshire?"

"They were. Not now they aren't. She's got them. Mrs.

175

Renton took them in an aeroplane."

David raised his eyes to the ceiling.

"Moira has her moments."

"Miss Blane was sick all the way," Pauline sobbed.

David laughed.

"I always seem to be mopping you up. You know, I told you before not to cry in London. It's particularly unlucky to-day, as I thought I'd take you round for a bite at the Aperitif, and I don't usually take ladies there with tear-smudges on their cheeks."

"Taking me!" She raised her head off his shoulder. "It's Pauline, you know. Did you think I was Petronella?"

He gave her behind an affectionate slap.

"Hop off and do something to your face. Of course I knew it was you. I can't see Peter shedding a tear even if on a coronation day she had sent the crown jewels to Balmoral instead of Buckingham Palace."

Pauline was so charmed to hear she was lunching with him, her tears stopped as if a tap had been turned off.

"I can't go just yet. I'm in charge till the others come back. There's nobody here but me."

"What about me?"

"You couldn't sell anything."

"I like that. After all, I designed the things. Scram."

They sat side by side at lunch. David made a pretence of asking her what she would eat, but she was in such a trance she would have agreed to anything.

"Steak Diane?" he suggested. "I think you need nourishing after so much emotion."

"Fancy," she replied, "I never expected you back to-day."

He looked at her with amusement.

"An important observation, but not one calculated to assist in the choice of food." He turned to the waiter. "Two steak Diane and two cocktails. A dry Martini for me, and a very mild one made with passion fruit juice for the lady."

"I can't drink a cocktail," Pauline expostulated.

"Yes you can. A mild one. You see in common decency we must drink a toast to the wedding."

Pauline's heart dropped like a stone. No wonder he was so gay. How odd Petronella hadn't told her.

He patted her hand.

"No need to look tragic. I rang up Moira while you were titivating. The clothes are all there. The hag looks almost nice, and the Duchess is so pleased she's given them champagne for lunch. If you knew how mean the Pulfords are you'd know what a triumph that is for my dress-designing—" He broke off and stared at her. "You are a funny person, Twin. Your eyes are shining as if the hag was your sister. What are you so pleased about?"

"I don't know," Pauline said evasively. "I'm just silly."

They had a cheerful lunch. The cocktail, mild though it was, seemed just the tonic Pauline needed after her morning. She grew gaily conversational. He asked all about the shop, and what had been ordered while he was away. One thing puzzled her. He never mentioned Petronella, and when she mentioned her he changed the subject.

"Did you have a nice holiday?" she asked him.

"Grand. Always a lot of fun those cricket tours."

"Did you make a lot of runs?"

"Not so bad towards the end. My eye was out at the beginning."

"That's why you said you needed a holiday. Is it back now?"

"I hope so. I haven't tried it out."

At the coffee stage he said suddenly:

"Could you dine with me this week?"

She put down her cup.

"I could, of course, because as a matter of fact I'm not going out at all. And I'd like to because I've got a new dress. It's the black net Petronella borrowed that time. It had a mark on it, but it's cleaned beautifully. But wouldn't you rather see Petronella first? I don't think she's got a night free, but she might put somebody off."

She couldn't see his face as he was looking down at the bill.

"I won't upset her plans. How about to-morrow night? It's time we got going on your schemes for the staff."

She wriggled with pleasure.

"Oh, good. I did hope you hadn't forgotten. I've another one that needs help, Mrs. Brown, she needs a holiday awfully, and she can't afford to go away and—"

He smiled at her. His voice was at its most gentle.

"I wonder how 'Reboux' managed till you came along. Funny we've been going some years and I've never before been asked to help any of them."

She pulled on her gloves.

"That's because you've never had a parson's daughter about. We're trained to it, you know. It's all right when we're young, but Mum says it's awful when we get old spinsters. It'll come so that I get putting my nose in where it isn't wanted."

He got up.

"Well, don't fuss about it yet. It's very useful where it is."

That evening when Moira got home from the wedding it

was only a quarter to six, so she dialled "Reboux's" number. David, she heard, was gone, but Miss Jones answered the phone. Yes, Mr. Bliss had been back. He had stayed till tea-time. No, he had not designed any clothes on the girls. No, he had not taken Peter to be photographed. He had sat alone in his office working on a drawing.

Moira put down her receiver and looked pleased. Perhaps he was cooling off. Anyway, it would not be so long now. The competition was only open one more week. By the end of the month the results should be out. Once out she'd take a bet he could whistle for Petronella.

Miss Jones also looked pleased as she put down her receiver.

"And you didn't ask who he lunched with, and you aren't going to know. But I'd give a lot to see your face if I told you."

CHAPTER 10

My dear Moira,

    It is the unanimous decision of the judges that your young woman is in the first fifty. Will you present her for inspection in a bathing-dress at Her Majesty's Theatre on Wednesday next at 2.30?

        Yours,
          R. N.

PS. Don't blame me if they turn her down. I've not seen her legs.

Moira read the note when she came in from the shop. She had taken it with her to work the next morning. The week-end came and she still had said nothing to Petronella. With an ordinary girl it would be easy, especially when you knew beforehand that they would be delighted to compete. But Petronella was such a fool. There was no reason to suppose she would not tell everybody. Even if she only told one person the affair would be finished and heaven knows how she would extricate herself, for David would be furious, let alone the child's parents. In the end she decided not to warn Petronella beforehand.

Much against the grain she spent a lot of money on an expensive bathing-dress. "Reboux" never had sold bathing-dresses, and she certainly could not draw attention to herself by stocking them in the autumn. Then she sent for

Miss Edwards and told her that she would need Petronella on Wednesday.

"I'm taking her to be photographed."

In answer to Miss Edwards' inquiry as to what clothes were to be packed, she chose some woollen suits as least likely to be harmed by being a long while in a box.

On Tuesday she sent for Petronella.

"I'm taking you to be photographed to-morrow afternoon. I shall want your hair specially dressed so I'll take you to my own hairdresser. Please be ready by eleven-thirty. I will give you a bite before the sitting."

Petronella met Miss Edwards.

"What on earth am I wearing for the photographs to-morrow? She's having my hair mucked about by her hairdresser for it. It's an awful bore, it was only washed two days ago."

"Hair washed!" Miss Edwards stared at her. "Are you sure? It's only the woollens, and you show a hat with those."

"I bet I don't." Petronella moved off gloomily. "It's going to be one of those awful out on the moors with the dogs affair I expect. I hate those sort of photographs, it takes me hours to get my hair right after them."

It was not till Moira had Petronella safely opposite her at lunch that she told her where she was going.

"Have you seen a competition in the *Sunday News* and in all the daily Nilk Press for the loveliest girl in the British Isles to be Miss Metropolis?"

"No." Petronella went on rummaging in the claw of a lobster for the meat. "I never read any but the film papers. Has somebody won it?"

"No, but somebody's going to of course."

Petronella succeeded in getting out the bit of lobster she was after.

"I bet they look like the hind legs of an elephant. They always do."

"I read of the competition some weeks ago," said Moira, marvelling that so few wits could go with so much beauty. "There's a large money prize, and as well the winner is having a test by a Hollywood film company."

"Lucky them."

Moira sighed. This was annoyingly uphill work.

"It might be lucky you."

"Oh, no, it couldn't. I never sent in a photograph."

"But I did. Listen, darling," Moira's voice was eager. "I think you're too lovely to be wasted in a shop. So I sent in one of your photographs. I heard the other day. You are picked as one of the fifty finalists. You are to go to Her Majesty's Theatre this afternoon."

"Gosh!" Petronella opened her eyes in startled amazement. "What am I to wear?"

"A bathing-dress. I've got it here."

Petronella was so stunned she felt unable to finish her lobster.

"It's lucky Daddy doesn't know."

"And he mustn't," said Moira urgently. "No one must know but just you and me. There's sure to be some more heats. And just suppose you were picked as a winner, you must have your film test before anyone interferes."

"Gosh!" said Petronella again, quite overcome by the glory of this vision. "A film test. Gosh!"

"But you won't get it," Moira pointed out, "if you say one

word about the competition to anybody. Somebody is sure to stop you having it."

The waiter took away the plates and brought round the trolley of sweets. Petronella chose a Mont Blanc of chestnut and cream. She stared at it dreamily.

"I'm not awfully good at not telling people things. There's so few interesting things to talk about that when I have got something to say I simply have to say it because there isn't anything else."

Moira could have slapped her.

"Well, that's all right. I've given you your chance, if you don't want it, it's up to you."

Petronella took a spoonful of her sweet.

"That's right," she agreed, when she'd swallowed it. "I will try, but things I think just come out. I never mean to say them."

Arriving at the theatre they were sent round to the stage door and put in a dressing-room with ten other girls. The ten other girls who had been politely chatting to each other, and the mothers of the ten other girls who had been pretending it was all fun and nobody cared who won, suddenly fell silent. All their eyes were glued on Petronella while she changed, and a friendliness that was not there before banded them together. There were some things which were not fair, and allowing Petronella to enter the competition was certainly one of them.

A male and female artist of great distinction, a famous female photographer, and a male dress-designer were the judges. They were sitting in the stalls together with the American film company's British representative, a Mr. Levisohn, and Sir Robert Nilk. On the stage were a clutter

183

of Nilk Press people. Some had cameras, some note-books, they all tried to look busier than they were so as to impress Sir Robert.

A very dapper young man, who was a kind of personal A.D.C. to Sir Robert, sent someone round the dressing-rooms for the fifty entrants. When the forty-nine and Petronella reached the side of the stage he gave them their orders. Each would answer to their names and receive a number, each in turn would come on to the stage, walk down a flight of steps they would see there, and then stand about as the judges might order.

Petronella was number twenty-six. Moira was in no way surprised that she was not attending when her name was called; she was in fact examining her bathing-dress. She pushed her forward, pinned the number on her, and stood her in her place in the line.

"What a moron!" she thought despairingly. "What can David see in the little nit-wit?"

"Now do let's get what we want clear," said the female artist to her fellow judges. "I take it we've got to forget all we know about beauty and choose something scraggy."

The male artist, who was an old man and had been a dog with the ladies in his day, sighed:

"People don't understand curves nowadays."

"Oh, dear, you naughty man," the dress-designer expostulated shrilly. "I faint if I see a curve."

"Better prop yourself up in your seat then," Sir Robert retorted dryly. "There's one or two Junoesque creatures coming, my young man tells me."

The photographer, who was young, pretty and sensible, settled back in her seat.

"I bet our standards of beauty don't differ all that much. Let's have them on. I dare say we can weed out the hopeless, and not start quarrelling about what makes for perfection until we get the last dozen or so. What do you think, Mr. Levisohn?"

Mr. Levisohn put another match to his cigar.

"My people are always looking for new types. I can give tests to any of them that look hopeful. Not that I ever knew anything that was any use for the screen come out of one of these competitions. But here's hoping."

"Right." Sir Robert picked up a megaphone. "We're ready here, Sappleworth."

The A.D.C. put a busy and humble face round a scenery flat.

"Right, Sir Robert." He turned to the entrants. "Are you ready, girls? Come on, number one."

"Of course," said the female artist to the photographer as number twenty-five appeared on the steps, "I can't think what you people do to them. All these creatures looked all right in their photographs."

"Terrible," groaned the dress-designer. "I shall be sick."

"Not so bad," said the male artist. "I do like rounded hips."

"They're not a very remarkable lot," said the photographer to Mr. Levisohn.

Mr. Levisohn looked up from the paper on which he was scribbling.

"Oh, I don't know. Number ten might make a comedy type. Lucky if I find anything."

"Next, Sappleworth," Sir Robert roared angrily into his megaphone.

"It isn't fair," said the mother of twenty-five to the mother of twenty-four. "They look much longer over some of the girls. If they hadn't been so quick they'd have seen what a lovely smile Bessie has."

"Come on, twenty-six," said the A.D.C. "Don't go to sleep."

Petronella came to herself with a start. She had been miles away indulging in a day-dream in which she not only won and got a film contract, but was actually in Hollywood meeting Robert Taylor. Her eyes still cloudy with the glory of that vision, she wandered on to the stage. She had forgotten the order about the stairs. She merely sauntered on and stood by the footlights smiling at the judges, wondering which of them was the film man.

The judges all sat up.

"Botticelli!" said the male artist.

"Don't be a fool," said the female one. "She's unique."

The photographer turned to Sir Robert:

"Did you ever as a child find yourself feeling stunned at the sight of a laburnum tree in full flower?"

"Queer you should say that." Sir Robert swallowed to hide his emotion. "Reminded me of when I was a boy. Flowers and things, you know."

"Oh, dear," said the dress-designer. "She's really too, too much. She oughtn't to be allowed."

"Gosh!" Petronella looked apologetically over the footlights. "I ought to be walking down those stairs, oughtn't I?"

"It's all right, my dear. Just stand as you are." Sir Robert's voice was so gentle that all the satellites of the Nilk Press looked round the flats to see if he was ill.

Mr. Levisohn stood up.

"If you don't mind, Sir Robert, I'd like her to move a bit. Just step up those stairs, dear, and as you come down say something to Sir Robert. Then turn round so that we can see your profile."

Petronella climbed to the top of the stairs.

"That is what I'm supposed to do at the shop," she explained cheerfully. "I'm not any good at it. I usually stumble. But I dare say I could learn."

"I'll arrange a test for that kid to-morrow," said Mr. Levisohn.

"I suppose we must see the other twenty-four?" the photographer queried.

"There are second and third to choose," reminded the male artist, who was enjoying himself.

"Can I go now?" asked Petronella. "Have you seen me all round?"

"Delicious creature," said the dress-designer. "I'm sure she's divinely idiotic."

"She can't go." Mr. Levisohn bustled out. "I must fix a time to shoot her."

"Of course she can't go," Sir Robert spluttered. "Must have her on again for the final heat. Sappleworth, take Miss—Miss—well, number twenty-six and make her comfortable. Haven't you a sofa she can rest on? And don't let the child hang about in draughts."

"It's stuffy, if anything," said Petronella. She looked at the A.D.C. "Shall I come off?"

The A.D.C., seeing which way the wind blew, and not at all surprised at its blowing, became all obsequiousness.

"Yes, please. This way. I'll fetch you when we want you.

Would you like some tea or anything?"

"Well, if you could get it, I would like a choc-bar," Petronella suggested. "I'm hot."

The A.D.C. beckoned to a Nilk satellite.

"A choc-bar. No, I don't know where you get one. Try the Savoy Hotel. Explain it's for a friend of Sir Robert."

The forty-nine mothers looked at each other. Nobody said a word. There are some wounds which go too deep for words.

Moira, seeing that she need not bother any more about Petronella, as the whole of the Nilk Press were fluttering round her, retired to a quiet corner with Mr. Levisohn.

"I'd like a test in the next few days," he said, offering her a cigarette. "Mr. Zilk is over here himself. I should like him to see it and make a decision before he goes back."

"It better be to-morrow." Moira leant against the wall. "It's all going to take a bit of handling. The child's well under age. And her family will be against it when they find out."

"Against it!" Mr. Levisohn stared at her. "But with that face and figure it might mean anything. Simply anything."

Moira nodded.

"I know. But the father's a parson, and from what I hear, isn't out for that sort of 'anything'. He thinks girls should marry and settle down."

"Then how——"

Moira winked.

"Make the test quickly, Mr. Levisohn. Get a decision at once. The results of this competition are to be out on Sunday. You'll have to hurry. Can it be done?"

Mr. Levisohn tapped his teeth thoughtfully.

"I think so. I'll telephone to Mr. Zilk now. Give me your phone number. I shall want her at the studio tomorrow."

David and Pauline were dining together. Since his holiday he had made a habit of asking her to dine with him about twice a week. He had given up asking Petronella to come out with him; Pauline thought she knew why. He probably imagined that Petronella would miss not being bothered by him and try harder. An almost motherly smile came over her face when she thought this. Men, she found, were very like little boys when it came to getting what they wanted. Full of secret ideas about the best way to do it. And most of the time it wasn't the best way at all. Certainly, if that was his plan, it wasn't working with Petronella, who had so many men wanting to entertain her she couldn't fit them in as it was. All the same, though she was sorry for him about Petronella, she was glad for herself. Her evenings with him were becoming nicer and nicer. They spent a lot of time over the plans for the people in the shop, and a lot when he told her about himself. She liked talking about him best, especially the part of his life when he had been small and bitter. She felt it was good for the small boy she had never known to be taken out into the light and have his bruises kissed and made well.

"I've a bit of news for you," David grinned. "I'll give you two guesses."

"Will I like it?"

"Yes."

"Is it to do with 'Reboux's?' "

"Yes. That's not guessing. Come on."

Pauline laid down her knife and fork and looked

thoughtful.

"If it's to do with the shop it's either about Miss Jones' mother—and it can't be that, because the only really good thing that could happen would be she shouldn't live, and you wouldn't say I'd like that. It can't be about Miss Blane, because your doctor only X-rayed her yesterday and he said he wouldn't let you know till next week. Brownsy has had her holiday, so it isn't her, and even you couldn't get her husband out of prison."

He laughed.

"It would be a doubtful kindness if I could."

"I know! It's Miss Edwards. You've got Tom a job."

He nodded.

"He's to see the people next week. It's with Butlers, the furniture people. Their special polishing fellow has to give up. It's a permanent job if he's any good."

Pauline was pink with pleasure.

"Goodness! I'm almost too happy to eat. I should think they'd put up their banns at once, wouldn't you? When will you tell her?"

"You shall do the telling. Then send her in to see me."

"Oh, dear, you are nice. She will be happy."

"It's your doing, not mine. I never knew there was a Tom. I'm only just beginning to take a real interest in my own shop." He fiddled with his bread. "Have you sold many frocks lately?"

Pauline stared at him.

"Quite a lot. I mean, I'm doing all right in the showroom, though I liked being runner better."

"What have you sold?"

"Three copies of the white marocain, and two of the

tweed three-piece. And the black model, and—"

"Could you remember the prices?"

"Of course."

He took a scrap of paper out of his pocket.

"Are those right?"

"No. There's eight guineas too little on the white marocains, and five on the tweeds, and ten on the black."

"I see." He put the paper back in his pocket.

She made a puzzled face.

"Don't you decide what they're going to cost?"

"Yes. Moira and I do. But I had a sudden idea that since I was taking a belated interest in the running of my establishment, I'd have a look at the books."

"Don't you usually?"

"No. Moira does them with some accountant friend of hers."

Pauline put her elbows on the table and rested her chin in her hands.

"Talking of her—do you ever get a feeling that there's something happening you don't know anything about?"

"I do. As a matter of fact, between you and me, that's why I want to look over the account books."

Pauline was shocked.

"I'm sure they're all right. Mrs. Renton is very good at sums and things like that, she'd never make a mistake. I meant just that things are queer."

"What d'you mean? Out with it, Twin."

"Well, it'll have to be a 'bought tell'."

"Is it anything I ought to interfere about?"

"No, you couldn't."

"Go ahead then. I'll buy it."

"Well, on Wednesday Mrs. Renton took Petronella to be photographed. They went in the morning because her hair had to be specially done. That was odd, because it was woollens and they're usually shown with hats. But that wasn't the oddest part. When they came back Miss Edwards gave me the box of clothes to unpack. Well, they hadn't been worn."

"How d'you know?"

"Because I packed them. We do, you know, in the showroom when it's things going to the photographer."

"My dear, all packing looks much alike, doesn't it?"

"Yes. But when I was packing the three-piece I found a button was loose. There wasn't time to send it to the workroom. So I packed it on the top and wrote on an old envelope, 'Be careful of the third button down or it'll come off.' Well, the envelope was just where I put it."

David made a puzzled face.

"What are you driving at? That they never went to the photographer?"

"Yes. I said to Petronella, 'Weren't you photographed to-day?' And she looked queer and said, just as if she'd learnt a lesson, 'Yes. And I shall be all day to-morrow'."

"That's very odd. What on earth's Moira up to? I shouldn't have thought Petronella was a liar."

"She's not. She'd never bother. Then she was so queer. You know nothing much makes her excited, but she was this time. I think it's something to do with Sunday."

"Why?"

"Because she said this morning that she felt tired and didn't think she'd go home for the week-end."

"Perhaps she is tired."

"Her! I said, 'Not a bit, you aren't.' And I'd promised Mum we'd always come and I'd send a telegram at once if she wasn't going to. Then she did a very odd thing. She said, 'Anyway, you'll be there. I do hate a fuss.' So I said, 'Fuss about what?' and she said she couldn't explain, and after all it was her own life, and why shouldn't she do what she liked? And that was odd because Petronella never says anything like that, so somebody has said it to her." She turned to David. "In fact, I feel in a proper fuss."

David said nothing, only his hand under the table patted her knee, which she found very pleasant and consoling. At last he looked up.

"I'll go down to my aunt's to-morrow. Whatever mess that little fool Peter has got into I feel confident she'll wriggle out of. But I won't have you bothered. You shoulder far too many troubles as it is. If anything goes wrong and I can help, ring me up and I'll be along in ten minutes."

Pauline felt her inside swelling with pleasure. She knew, of course, that his calling Petronella a fool did not mean he was any less fond of her. She knew that his saying he was coming down because he wouldn't have her bothered was just an excuse to be near Petronella in case she needed him. But it was nice to hear him say he was coming because of her. Pretence was better than no affection at all.

He leant back in his chair.

"The day after the woollens were supposed to be photographed did Peter go out again to be photographed?"

Pauline nodded.

"All day. She took a box of all sorts of clothes."

"Had they been unpacked?"

She turned her eyes on him in hurt surprise.

"I wouldn't have thought you'd think I'd do a thing like that. I specially didn't undo the parcel and I never asked her anything about the day. Mrs. Renton took her at nine o'clock. And they didn't get back till six."

He lit a cigarette.

"If you thought something wrong was going on wouldn't you think it right to find out by any means what was happening?"

Pauline considered the point.

"Petronella wouldn't do anything wrong. Only silly."

"But suppose it was somebody else than Petronella?"

"Well, I'd much rather just ask them. I think snooping about finding things out is pretty mean."

David beckoned a waiter for his bill.

"You're too honest for this world, Paul. There are people who would only answer with lies."

"Well, I wouldn't snoop," she said stubbornly. "I'd tell them what I thought."

"Would you despise me if I didn't?"

She knew that nothing could make her despise him.

"I never despise people."

"You're a funny child," he said softly. "The first time I saw you I wished to be back at the golden age. Now I wish it more than ever. People who've lost their faculties by growing up have very little to offer you."

She picked up her bag.

"I'm quite grown-up really." She walked up the restaurant. "Awful how country cousin I seem to him," she thought. "No wonder it's Petronella he loves."

Moira was dining with Mr. Levisohn.

"It's all fixed," she said. "My maid has booked rooms at the Bliss Arms for you and me. There's going to be a fight."

Mr. Levisohn turned over his caviare.

"Most girls can persuade their parents into doing what they want."

"Not this one. She's quite blah. Not that I mean she won't make a very good actress," she added hurriedly.

"Sex-appeal girls don't want to be good actresses," said Mr. Levisohn. "When a woman thinks, she gets lines. I'd reckon that girl has never had five minutes clear thinking in her life."

"You're right there, that's why we've got to be on the spot when the papers come out . . . She'll just subside left to herself. I've told her to phone the moment trouble starts and we'll be at the Vicarage in a few minutes."

"I never had much dealings with the clergy," said Mr. Levisohn. "But I dare say they understand hard cash talk like ordinary men."

"Some do, some don't." Moira watched the waiter remove their caviare plates. "From what I can glean from Peter this is one of the don'ts."

Mr. Levisohn felt the champagne to see it was cool enough.

"Well, he's got to be talked into it or I'm out on my jacksy. When Mr. Zilk saw that test I thought he was going mad. 'Buy her,' he said. And when Mr. Zilk says 'buy' it's just too bad for someone if they can't."

Moira picked up her glass and sipped her champagne. She would have preferred brandy, but Mr. Levisohn was a man who thought champagne the only drink on the menu.

195

And this was very good champagne.

"Well, here's to crime and our rake-off on the girl's earnings."

Mr. Levisohn took a sip.

"Here's to crime," he agreed. "But I don't like rake-offs mentioned at dinner."

CHAPTER 11

IT WAS SUNDAY morning. Mark, getting up at half-past six, looked out of his dressing-room window and saw it was pouring with rain. He did not sigh for his bed with criticism of the powers above, he did just regret how often it had to rain on Sundays.

At seven the maid, Alice, got up and went down to make a cup of tea for the cook. While she was busy with the kettle the milkman arrived. The maid took the milk, observing it was a dirty day.

"Not half," agreed the milkman. "It's cold too."

"Well," said Alice, "come in and have a cup of tea. It'll warm you."

Over a congenial cup she heard the local gossip.

"There's people come to the Bliss Arms," said the milkman, stirring his tea. "One's a titled lady, Honourable Mrs. something, but she doesn't seem no connection with her ladyship."

Alice was properly interested.

"That's queer. If she's not here to see Lady Bliss, what is she here for?"

"The landlord said as he had a word with her maid, Ida her name is, a nice young person but close. But as far as he could make out she didn't know why they were there no more than we do. She said coming to the country in the autumn wasn't her idea of fun."

"My!" said Alice. "Interesting, isn't it? I'll ask Miss Petronella. She always finds out what's going on."

"Talking of Miss Petronella—*he's* up at the Manor

again." He gave Alice a nudge to show they were discussing a love-affair.

"No! Keeping it dark this time. He hasn't been down here, nor he hasn't telephoned."

"Reckon that's a case."

"Hope so," Alice agreed. "He's a nice gentleman."

"Talking of gentlemen," said the milkman, "there's a gentleman staying at the Arms too."

"With the lady?"

"No, nothing like that. Quite separate, though the maid booked for them both."

"Go on," said Alice.

"Who's thinking things?" the milkman retorted. The rest of the tea-drinking passed very happily in a I-don't-mean-what-you-mean conversation.

For practically the only time in her life Petronella had not slept well. That is to say she had woken twice in the night, turned on the light, once seen it was four and the other time six, said, "Oh, gosh, it's Sunday," and turned over and gone to sleep again.

At half-past seven she had woken for good. She sat up in bed and found it was cold. She spent the next ten minutes wishing that somebody was about to light the gas-fire for her. At the end of that time she rather crossly put on her dressing-gown and lit it herself. She looked out of the window and saw the rain.

"Gosh," she thought, "it would rain." She shivered. She analysed nothing, so she supposed the shiver was cold, so got back into bed. Actually it was nerves.

"I wish the paper had come," she thought, "and it was over. I do hate a fuss, and there's sure to be an awful fuss about this. I do hope it isn't a very big picture of me, then perhaps nobody will see it. If they don't see it Daddy mightn't ever know. After all, we don't take that paper, so somebody's got to tell him. But anyway I'll have to tell him about Hollywood. Goodness, there will be a row. I wonder if Pauline's awake. I might go in and talk to her. It's like waiting for the dentist being here alone."

In the passage Petronella met Catherine hurrying down the stairs to early service. She stopped to kiss her daughter.

"You're up early, darling. Why don't you ask Alice for some tea? It's a long time before breakfast."

Petronella went into Pauline's room. Pauline was awake.

"Hullo," she said. "What's up?"

"Nothing. I was awake, so I came to see if you were."

Petronella got into the bed. "You might go down and get Alice to make us some tea."

"Why don't you go if you want it?"

"I feel queer inside." Petronella lay flat on her back. "Every few minutes part of me seems to go cold."

"Where?"

"In the middle of me."

Pauline looked at her sister.

"You look all right, but I don't mind going for the tea." She pulled on her dressing-gown. "You haven't done something you're worrying about, have you?"

" 'Course not," said Petronella crossly. "Do go on and get that tea."

Pauline went down to the kitchen. Neither Alice nor cook were visible, but Pauline could hear them at the back door talking to what appeared to be the whole of Alice's family. She went out and joined them.

"Is anything wrong?"

Cook turned round to her. She held a newspaper.

"It depends who calls what wrong," she said grimly. "But I'd like to know what the Vicar will say. Did you know about this, Miss Pauline?"

Pauline took the paper. Petronella's hopes for a small photograph had not been realized. The entire front page was one enormous portrait of her head. Over it was written, "NEW BEAUTY QUEEN FOR LONDON." And under that, "MISS PETRONELLA LANE WINS TITLE OF MISS METROPOLIS AND HOLLYWOOD CONTRACT." At the bottom it said, "For Miss Lane's life-story, and pictures of other prize-winners, see page six."

"Isn't it wonderful, Miss?" gasped Alice. "Fancy, Hollywood! Don't I wish I was her!"

"I saw it when the papers come to the shop," piped up Alice's brother, "and I run straight home with it to Mum and Dad."

"And I said better take it to the Vicarage," said Alice's father, who was a sidesman. "I thought maybe the Vicar didn't know, Miss Pauline. It doesn't seem the sort of thing he'd hold with."

"Still, it's a wonderful chance," Alice's mother broke in. "I dare say it'll all work out for the best."

"It's what Mr. Bliss'll do, I'm wondering," said Alice sentimentally.

Pauline looked at them all wild-eyed. What had Petronella done? No wonder she hadn't wanted to be home this week-end. How could any of them tell Father? It was the kind of thing he thought disgusting. He was funny and old-fashioned about women. He thought they needed

200

sheltering and looking after, and had said, over and over again, that the way they were always being pushed forward was spoiling them as wives and mothers. What on earth would he think then of his daughter having her picture on a whole page of the paper? "New Beauty Queen for London." What would poor David think? What would he do if Petronella really went to Hollywood? Clutching the paper she ran out of the kitchen and up the stairs.

"It's plain she's upset," said Cook to Alice and her family. "And she won't be the only one, you mark my word. It's not at all the goings-on you expect in a vicarage."

Petronella saw Pauline's face and the paper. She looked at her over the top of the sheets with scared eyes.

"It wasn't my idea, it was Mrs. Renton's."

"You'll have to stop it at once," said Pauline. "Daddy will hate it."

"I shan't stop it." Petronella sounded quite firm for her. "I've always wanted to go to Hollywood, and now I'm going."

"But Daddy'll die."

"It's my life." Petronella looked as if she were going to cry. "Couldn't I stop in bed all day and not come down till the fuss is over?"

Pauline was really annoyed.

"I like that. You go and get yourself made a beauty queen and then expect not to have to put up with the row. If I were you I'd get up at once and catch Mum when she comes in from church and tell her. It'll be better than her seeing this."

"Let me look." Petronella held out her hand. "Gosh!" Her voice was admiring. "Isn't it a gorgeous photograph?"

201

"Instead of lying there admiring yourself you'd better get up."

Petronella had turned to her life-story on page six.

"Listen. Miss Lane is the daughter of the Reverend Mark Lane of—"

"Will you shut up and get up," Pauline stormed. "Daddy isn't the only one who's going to mind. There's David."

"Why should he care? He can easily get another model. Oh, do listen. 'Of course, like all girls, I love films,' said little Miss Lane. 'But I never thought of a film career. It's like a fairy-story'."

"I bet you never said that." Pauline began dragging off her pyjamas. "If you won't go and tell Mum, I suppose I must. But I think it's frightfully mean."

Pauline, in spite of the wet, met her mother at the gate of the churchyard.

"My dear," said Catherine, "what are you doing out here in all this rain?"

"Mum." Pauline hung on to her arm. "Something awful's happened. Petronella has gone in for a beauty competition. It wasn't her idea, it was Mrs. Renton's. But she's won it and got a film contract. And"—her voice fell to a shocked whisper—"her photograph is all over the Sunday paper."

In one quick flash Catherine saw all the trials ahead of her. She knew far better than Pauline could imagine just how badly this would hit Mark. But being a wife and mother on a small income is strengthening to courage. She managed to smile.

"Well, it's not your fault, darling. Come along in and get that wet coat off and have some breakfast. Daddy won't be in for half an hour. By then I'll have thought out how best to tell him. Then we must see how we can get hold of Uncle Jim, he's a clever solicitor, he'll know best how to get Petronella out of this mess with as little fuss as possible. There must be lots of other girls who'd like to be beauty queens. I expect it can be arranged."

"But, Mum, you don't understand. Petronella's pleased. She wants to go to Hollywood."

"Well, she can't. She's under age. Don't look so worried, darling."

Catherine had intended to leave telling Mark until after he had eaten his breakfast, but such news as Petronella's fame had never touched the village before. Mark came in with an anxious frown.

"Catherine, come to my study a moment," he called. Catherine looked at Pauline. (Petronella had refused to come down.)

"Somebody has told him."

"Goodness," said Pauline, "I wouldn't be you for a lot."

"What's this they were telling me in the vestry about Petronella having won some beauty competition?"

Catherine went over to Mark. She took his hands.

"How cold you are. It's true, I'm afraid. The silly child went in for something, she's to be Miss Metropolis, or rather that's the title she's won. I'm ringing up Jim after breakfast. I've no doubt he'll settle it in a minute."

Mark looked at her with grief-stricken eyes.

"How horrible! It makes me feel my work has been wasted. What will my people feel when they read this about my daughter? How can I get up in the pulpit and beg for the simple things, talk of the wonder of home-life, when these things can happen in my own family? A beauty

203

queen! The vulgarity of it."

"I think," said Catherine gently, "this isn't a time to talk of ourselves or the effect we make on the outside world. The question is Petronella. She's won a contract to be a film actress in Hollywood. She wants to go."

"A film actress! She wants to be one?"

Catherine had to smile.

"You know, darling, you're being just a bit out of date. Girls do want these things."

"You don't want her to go?"

"Of course not. The whole thing must be cleared up as quietly as possible, but I do think we've got to think of Petronella. You are a parson and I do see how bad the effect of this vulgarity is on the younger people. But more important than your parish is your daughter. She's being offered—apparently begged—to earn vast sums, and you can't just say 'No'. We've got to be terribly tactful."

"As a clerk in Holy Orders my first duty is my people. My family, even you, must come second."

"Well, accepting that, what more can we do than get hold of Jim and get him to get us out of this muddle?"

"You can do that, my dear." Mark moved to the door. "I'll see Petronella. Where is she? I should like to be able to tell everybody that she is as distressed as we are, and has no intention of going on with the business."

Catherine shook her head despairingly.

"She's in bed. You'd far better have breakfast. She isn't distressed. In fact, she's pleased."

"Now I'm in for it," thought Petronella, staring with large eyes at her father.

Petronella at all times looked divine. In bed she looked

204

not only divine, but as unsmackable as a kitten. Even Mark found it hard to speak his mind. He sat down beside her.

"My child, this is a very distressing business."

"Well, it all depends how you look at things. I think it's fun. I always wanted to go to Hollywood, and I'm going to earn an awful lot of money."

"There is absolutely no talk of your going to Hollywood any more than we should think of allowing you to go on with this vulgar beauty queen business."

"Well, I thought you'd say that." Petronella flushed, for never in her life had she been defiant In fact, she had no need to be. "But all the same, I'm going. I don't mind a bit about being the beauty queen, that sounds dull, but I do want to go to Hollywood, and I've got a contract and you can't stop me."

To Mark his children were still little girls. They were still at the age when sweets could comfort any trouble. This idea had been shaken on the fatal Sunday when Catherine had persuaded him to let them work in London. He had felt then that London was no place for his children, and how right he had been. Now Petronella's defiance was to him the defiance of a naughty child.

"That's enough, Petronella. You will make Mummy and me very unhappy if you argue. Everything is settled. Your Uncle Jim is being asked to come here and he will get you free from this horrible business as soon as possible. Meanwhile my little girl must—"

"Oh, shut up," said Petronella, goaded past politeness. "There you sit saying 'you can't go' as if I'd asked to go to a bazaar or something. I've got a contract for Hollywood; it's for an awful lot of money; it's in dollars and so I forget what it is in pounds, but it's a lot. Of course I'm going. I should think even you would want to see people like Clark Gable and Bette Davis if you got the chance."

Clark Gable and Bette Davis meant nothing to Mark, but the talk of money horrified him.

"Don't I give you all you need, my darling?"

"Of course you don't. I don't want to be mean, but we earn what we have, and it's pretty awful never having enough clothes or anything."

"I'm sorry." Mark's voice was hurt and puzzled. "I must see what I can do. But you can't go to Hollywood."

"Can't! I can. I'm going."

Mark laid his hand on her hair.

"We'll have some more talks when you are less excitable. But put all thoughts of Hollywood out of your mind. You are under age. I shouldn't dream of allowing it."

In all Petronella's life she had never really wanted anything very fiercely. Such few things as she did want she had always succeeded someway in getting. Now, for the first time, she was up against a pointblank refusal. Her disappointment (though part of her refused to believe she wouldn't get her own way) was shattering. She burst into tears. Not decent, quiet sobs, but loud, child-like, disappointed howls.

Catherine and Pauline were still at the breakfast table. They jumped up.

"Poor Mark," said Catherine. "He ought not to have to put up with this on a Sunday. And he hasn't had any breakfast."

"Poor Petronella." Pauline ran to the door. "David's with Lady Bliss. I'll ring him up. He said he'd come if he was needed, and it looks as if he was."

"Oh, my!" said Cook to Alice. "I thought we'd have trouble."

Alice gazed wide-eyed at the roof where the howls were getting louder and more hysterical.

"Poor Miss Petronella. It's a shame if they don't let her take her prize."

Catherine found Mark ineffectually patting any bit of Petronella he could see, but Petronella had dived under the sheets to abandon herself to woe, and Mark's pats only received a convulsive shudder and kick which left his hand doing nothing.

"Come down to breakfast." Catherine put her hand through his arm. "It's no good talking to anybody when they're making that noise."

Mark looked sadly at the heaving bed, and heard the piercing cries. Then, obediently and half-stunned by noise, followed Catherine out.

Almost as the door closed Petronella looked out from under the sheets. She was still howling, but she abated the noise a little as she had no audience and crying alone wasn't much fun.

"Goodness," she hiccupped to herself, "how can they be so mean—I did so want to see Greta Garbo, and now I never will. Nobody told me if you were under age you couldn't go. Mrs. Renton said . . ."

And on that thought her tears stopped. Mrs. Renton! She and that polite Mr. Levisohn were at the Bliss Arms. "Ring me up if there's trouble," Moira had said.

Faintly sobbing, Petronella hurried down to the hall. To her disgust Pauline was on the phone.

"Give that to me," she sniffed. "It's awfully important."

Pauline looked round.

"So's this. It's to David. The butler's gone to fetch him."

"What good will he do?"

"Well, if you can't go to Hollywood you could—"

She broke off before she could lay her matrimonial scheme before Petronella. David's voice came over the phone.

"Hullo," said Pauline. "Is that you? Oh, please come. It's awful. Even worse than I thought."

David sounded amused.

"I've seen the paper. She seems to have done pretty well for herself."

"But Daddy won't let her be it—I mean, not a beauty queen, and he won't let her go to Hollywood."

"Dear me! Well, I'll come along at once. Don't fuss, Twin."

Pauline had hardly put down the receiver before Petronella snatched it up.

"Oh, please, I want to speak to Mrs. Renton. Yes, it's Miss Petronella. Please tell her to be very quick. Thank you. Yes, it is a nice photograph." There was a pause, then she quavered, "Is that you, Mrs. Renton? Oh, please come. Daddy won't let me go to Hollywood. Please be very quick."

The drawback to any comfort coming from the arrival of Moira, Mr. Levisohn and David was that Mark was shut in his study meditating before his service. He could not conceive that any of them had anything to do with his daughter's life. Fathers decided their children's future. He didn't so much refuse discussion as think it out of the question that anybody could have the impertinence to try and interfere.

Catherine, amazed at the number of people suddenly congregated in the house, coped as well as she could. In the charity of her nature she was prepared to believe that Moira had honestly meant kindly in sending in Petronella's photograph to the Nilk Press, and also took it for granted that she would be embarrassed when she realized that she had made a blunder. Mr. Levisohn she found more puzzling. His constant references to somebody called Mr. Zilk confused her. To David she turned as the drowning clutch at a reed. His reason for being there was clear and right. He wanted to marry Petronella. He must be as upset, perhaps more so than Mark. To him she was all gentleness.

"Now," said Mr. Levisohn. "I think the best thing I can do is to go right in to Mr. Lane and show him the contract."

"You can't do that," said Catherine, shocked. "He's thinking. He always does before he preaches."

"Well, then, I'll wait outside his study and catch him when he comes out. Maybe there's some little clause he doesn't like, but Mr. Zilk isn't a quibbler. 'What's a thousand here or there to me?' he always says."

"That's very nice of Mr. Zilk," said Catherine politely. "But it's not money. My husband just doesn't want her to go. She's too young."

"Ah!" Mr. Levisohn came and sat beside Catherine. "That's the very thing Mr. Zilk wants me to explain to Mr. Lane. You may think you take care of her, but it's nothing to the way Zilk Productions Limited feel." He lowered his voice. "Have to be strict. There's nothing makes a star slip like scandal."

"She couldn't go alone of course," put in Moira. "Perhaps you—"

Catherine laughed.

"She isn't going at all. But if she were I certainly wouldn't go with her. I can't think of anybody who could be more out of place than I'd be in Hollywood."

"I can go alone quite well," said Petronella, "if you all wouldn't fuss so."

"It's a pity she can't go next week. Mr. and Mrs. Zilk are going back on the *Queen Mary*," Mr. Levisohn broke in. "She couldn't do better than travel with Mrs. Zilk."

"Well, she can't," said Moira. "She has to be crowned at the newspapers' fair on Monday week."

"Crowned!" Catherine gasped.

"Yes. As the beauty queen 'Miss Metropolis'." Moira, to David's ear, was obviously intending Catherine should take this speech in. "Then when the fair's over she is to make appearances in all the big industrial towns. The mayor will meet her."

"Really, Moira," David looked at her with disgust. "Did you know all this had to happen? You must have been mad."

"I'm trying to get hold of a relation who's a solicitor," said Catherine. "He must see the newspaper people and explain she can't do it."

"It'll cost a lot," Moira lit a cigarette. "There's been a lot of money spent on the campaign. I should think Sir Robert would take the case to court."

"Oh, he couldn't!" Catherine turned white. "We've no money to fight a newspaper. But really we couldn't have her being crowned as a beauty queen. My husband has

210

always preached against that sort of thing. Oh, Mrs. Renton, if you only knew the trouble you've caused."

David nodded comfortingly to Catherine.

"Don't worry, we'll get her out of it."

"It's all very well to talk," Moira protested. "It's not going to be so easy."

David fixed her with his eyes.

"She is going to get out, and you, my sweet, who pushed her in, are going to do the pulling out."

"Am I?"

"Yes," David gave her a nod. "Or you're going to find yourself in something that nobody can pull you out of."

"Oh, really—" said Catherine, flustered at his tone. "I'm sure Mrs. Renton didn't mean—"

"I don't mind anybody getting me out of being a beauty queen," Petronella pointed out. "But I won't be got out of going to Hollywood."

"That's different." David, who was standing by her, put his arm round her. "I want to talk with your mother before anything's fixed about that."

Pauline looked at them with a pain in her heart. She didn't think Petronella would think being married much of a compensation for not going to Hollywood, but perhaps if the trousseau was grand enough, and the honeymoon somewhere very gay, she might agree.

Catherine gave David a dazzling smile. She knew, she thought, just what he was going to suggest. It was the solution, of course. In a big wedding all this trouble would be forgotten.

The study door opened. Mark had a great ability for throwing off his personal cares when it was a time to set apart for meditation and prayer.

He came out now with the aloof look of one who had been out of the world. It was so marked it even froze the words on Mr. Levisohn's lips.

Catherine came over and touched his arm.

"Mr. Bliss, Mrs. Renton and Mr. Levisohn are here about Petronella."

Mark recalled himself to the Vicarage. He looked at them all with a rather abstracted stare. Then he turned away.

"They'll all be coming to church, I suppose. I'll see them afterwards."

There was never an odder party in a vicarage pew. Moira hadn't been inside a church except for weddings and funerals since her own wedding. The simple sincerity of the service made her embarrassed and introspective.

Mr. Levisohn was a professing Jew. He attended to the service devoutly, and with the perspicacity of his race understood from Mark's spiritual fervour that perhaps there were people to whom money still meant very little. It depressed him. What chance had he and Mr. Zilk with people of such a viewpoint?

Petronella heard no word of the service. Remarkably unconscious of the interested eyes of all the parishioners fixed on her, she spent a happy time meeting on intimate terms those gorgeous creatures whom she only knew now through their films.

Pauline sat next to David. Once or twice during the service she caught his eye and when that happened she returned to her prayer-book or hymn-book glowing. This fuss seemed to have brought them very close together.

Mark gave the Blessing.

"The grace of our Lord Jesus Christ, and the love of God, and the fellowship of the Holy Ghost, be with us all evermore. Amen."

The congregation streamed out. David took hold of Catherine's elbow.

"Could I have a talk with you before the storm breaks, Mrs. Lane?"

Catherine met Mark in the garden. It had stopped raining and though it was cold it was not too cold to take him to look at the iris stylosa.

"Mr. Bliss has been talking to me about Petronella," she said while she fumbled amongst the grey-green stalks for the flowers and to feel if there was a thickening which meant buds. "He says we'll have to let Petronella go to Hollywood."

"I—"

She stopped him.

"He says, and I see he's right, that she'll go sooner or later, anyway. And if she goes now she has more chance to do really well."

"Why should she go sooner or later?"

"She's unusually lovely and she's set her heart on it."

Mark groaned.

"It's this dreadful beauty queen business, too."

Catherine showed him the buds on the irises.

"Fourteen. And there'll be a whole lot more soon. He says she needn't be a beauty queen. He's seeing that Mrs. Renton. He says he knows a way to make her get Petronella out of it. He says the excuse will have to be that she's leaving for America at once."

"It's out of the question."

"I know it seems so now." Catherine rubbed her cheek against his overcoat. "But perhaps it's meant to be, and when you've thought about it, you'll see a way."

Moira was in her sitting-room at the Bliss Arms. David stood opposite to her.

"You'll go to Sir Robert this afternoon. You'll tell him he's got to have it in all his papers tomorrow that Petronella's father disapproves of beauty competitions and in any case the girl is leaving at once for Hollywood."

"It mightn't be so easy."

"It should be for you. I suspect it's more or less what you planned should happen."

Moira looked up at him with all the charm she had in her.

"And what, do I get for arranging this?"

He came close to her. He looked right down at her, holding her chin so that she couldn't move.

"Nothing. You're a double-crossing twister, aren't you? I've been going through the books. I would have warned you only you weren't in the shop on Saturday. My God, the money you've made out of 'Reboux'. You're out, of course. I should send somebody to-morrow for your things. As for this scheme of getting that kid to America, I suspect you wanted to get her out of the way. I can't think you wanted to marry me, but perhaps you liked my money. But this time you've been too sharp and missed something that was sticking out a mile."

Moira jerked her head out of his hand.

"My God!" Then she shrugged her shoulders. "Unless you're inviting yourself to lunch you'd better hurry. Don't you have roast beef at one at the Manor?"

She watched the door shut, then she did a thing she hadn't done for years. She cried.

"Blast her," she sobbed. "Why didn't I spot that? Blast her."